Dear Reader:

I am so excited to present to you *The Street Sweeper*, the sequel to *Harlem's Dragon*. I am sure many of you will recognize the incredibly sexy cover model from movies like Tyler Perry's *Madea's Family Reunion*. Yes, he was the stripper dressed as a police officer. He is hot and so is the author of this book: David Rivera, Jr.

Rivera has penned yet another powerful tale involving Chemah, a police detective of both African American and Latino descent, who is not only all about doing his job right but also doing his women right. This time he finds himself challenged with both a serial killer dubbed "The Street Sweeper" who has no conscience and apparently no plan to stop murdering people in cold blood. He also finds himself caught up with a new love; a blind woman who not only does not consider herself handicapped but uses her lack of sight to build strength in many other ways.

If you enjoyed *Harlem's Dragon* you will love this novel. In fact, you will love this novel even if you did not read the prequel, but make sure that you ultimately read both. Thank you for supporting Mr. Rivera's efforts and thank you for supporting one of the dozens of authors published under my imprint, Strebor Books. I try my best to bring you cutting-edge works of literature that will keep your attention and make you think long after you turn the last page.

If you are interesting in making extra income, please email dante@strebor books.com to be sent an "Opportunity" packet. Now sit back in your favorite chair or, better yet, chill in the bed, and be prepared to be tantalized by yet another great read.

Peace and Many Blessings,

Zane

Publisher
Strebor Books International
www.streborbooks.com

ZANE PRESENTS

David Rivera, Jr.

The Street Sweeper

SEE NO EVIL

SBI

STREBOR BOOKS

NEW YORK LONDON TORONTO SYDNEY

Strebor Books
P.O. Box 6505
Largo, MD 20792
http://www.streborbooks.com

The Street Sweeper © 2006 by David Rivera, Jr.

ISBN-13 978-1-59309-100-2
ISBN-10   1-59309-100-1
LCCN 2006928392

Distributed by Simon & Schuster, Inc.
1230 Avenue of the Americas
New York, NY 10020
1-800-223-2336

First Strebor Books trade paperback edition October 2006

10 9 8 7 6 5 4 3 2

Manufactured and Printed in the United States of America

For information regarding special discounts for bulk purchases, please contact Simon & Schuster Special Sales at 1-800-456-6798 or business@simonandschuster.com

DEDICATION

This book is dedicated to my father, Jose "Chemah" Melendez,
who showed me how to laugh in the face of adversity
and rise above the petty worries of life.

ACKNOWLEDGMENTS

I will always be thankful to Grandmaster Sam McGee and Master Dwayne McGee who are the true Heroes and Champions of Harlem's youth.

Thanks to Ryan Gentles who lent his regal presence on the cover.

Peace to Zane and Charmaine at Strebor for giving me continued opportunities to grow.

Thanks to John Gonzalez for once again capturing the image that adds a thousand words to my thousand words.

To all the people in my life who make me laugh and make me cry, thank you.

"There is only one happiness in life, to love and be loved."
—GEORGE SAND

Prayer:

May the evil man be good.
May the good man find peace.
May he who finds peace be free.
And may he who is free make others free.

Chapter 1
RITE OF PASSAGE

The echo of Chemah's footsteps rang on deaf ears as he walked along the cobblestone streets under the West Side Highway and 125th Street. He was walking the crime scene as per usual, trying to get a feel for what had transpired. He looked down the road at the Fairway supermarket less than a block and a half away and wondered how it was possible that no one had seen the body of this poor woman being dumped here.

Chemah had been at his son Tatsuya's school when he received the call to come to the scene. Tatsuya had been in another fight or, as Chemah saw it, another ass whuppin'. Tatsuya, now nine years old and in the fourth grade, was sitting on a wooden bench in the principal's office when Chemah reached the school. He was sporting a dirty face with a fat lip when Chemah was escorted in by the secretary. Sitting next to him was another little boy of about the same age, but of a slightly smaller stature. The smaller boy smiled up sweetly at Chemah as he entered the room and Chemah knew that this was the boy who had damaged Tatsuya.

"Good afternoon, Mr. Rivers," the principal said, acknowledging Chemah from behind her desk as he came toward her.

"What's happening now?" Chemah said, exasperated at seeing his only son brutalized by a child smaller than him.

"Will you boys wait outside," the principal said, directing the two boys sitting on the bench toward her door. Mrs. Whales waited a moment for the boys to shut it before attempting to explain the situation.

When they were alone, she turned to Chemah. "Tatsuya has been fighting again, Mr. Rivers. Or more to the point, he's been getting beaten up. As you know by now he refuses to defend himself against the other boys who've been giving him a hard time."

Chemah was fuming. "Can't you control those little...little...?" Chemah was at a loss for words.

Mrs. Whales took a deep, anguished breath before she began to speak again. "Mr. Rivers, it pains me to say this and if you ever quote me, I'll deny having said it, but drastic times call for drastic measures." Chemah's ears became instantly alert. He was afraid he knew what she was going to say next. "Have you tried teaching Tatsuya to defend himself if someone lashes out at him? The truth is he has set himself up as such a target that just about any child with an ounce of malicious intent could assault him. I can only do so much to protect him, if he won't speak up for himself." She had said exactly what Chemah was afraid of.

In point of fact Chemah had no need to teach Tatsuya to defend himself. Tatsuya and he both belonged to the largest and arguably the best karate school in Harlem. Tatsuya was one of the better fighters in his age group and Chemah held the rank of master in the school.

He'd already had countless talks with Tatsuya regarding his unwillingness to defend himself and he was frustrated that none of the talks had borne fruit. "I'll have a talk with him," Chemah said, unwilling to go into the topic of self-defense.

He already felt inadequate enough as a single father. It was hard raising two children alone. He had very little family in the city and both his children required a lot of attention.

His cellphone rang as Mrs. Whales raised another question that would provoke his internal barometer. "Do you think Tatsuya could benefit from a mentoring program?" she asked.

Chemah held up his index finger, indicating she should hold that thought as he flipped open his phone. Chemah listened intently to whoever was at the other end of the conversation and then responded, "I'll be right there," and closed his phone. "Excuse me, but I have to go," he said abruptly to Mrs. Whales. Mrs. Whales understood the importance of the phone call Chemah had taken. She knew from the newspapers that Chemah was one of the most cele- brated detectives in New York City. He had helped solve homicides that had perplexed other detectives. She still remembered reading the article that described the tragedy in his personal life: he'd had to arrest his own wife on murder charges. A later article mentioned that she was eventually convicted of manslaughter and sentenced to five years in the penitentiary.

Chemah had been left to take care of a newborn baby girl and his son, who at the time had been only five years old.

Mrs. Whales felt the need to talk to Chemah further concerning Tatsuya, but realized he did not take his parental responsibilities lightly. If he said he had to leave, it must be really important. She nodded her head in understanding and walked him to her office door.

When Chemah opened the door, he saw a Hispanic-looking woman talking to the young man with whom Tatsuya had had the altercation. Chemah assumed it was the boy's mother. *She doesn't look angry at the little boy*, Chemah thought. *She's probably secretly proud that he beat up a bigger boy.* The thought made Chemah angry and he gave the lady a dirty look.

He went to the seat where Tatsuya sat looking forlorn and bent down on one knee in front of him. "How you doing, big man?" he said, trying to conjure up a smile.

Tatsuya touched his swollen bottom lip gingerly with two fingers. "It doesn't hurt that bad, Dad."

"I know, I know it doesn't hurt you. You're a tough guy," Chemah said, mussing Tatsuya's hair. Tatsuya's face broke into a full unabashed smile. "Listen, I have to go to work now. I may not be back from work till late, so I'm going to need you to help out with Héro while I'm out, okay?"

Tatsuya nodded his head vigorously. When his father gave him an assign- ment, he took it seriously. Before Tatsuya's mother had died and he came to live with his father and stepmother, Tatsuya had been a very happy child. He had started to have a semblance of a normal life again when his stepmother was arrested for causing the death of his mother. Now he rarely trusted anyone other than his father. Chemah knew this and could find no way to fight the boy's reasoning. He himself struggled with the same problem.

The only unaffected one was Héro, his three-year-old daughter. She was always happy. Tatsuya and Chemah spoiled her rotten. Tatsuya was especially protective of the little girl. He insisted on doing everything for her, even when they had a babysitter.

Having said all he could to the boy right now without getting into a lecture, Chemah kissed Tatsuya on top of the head and stood up to leave.

Chemah had walked out of the principal's office and several yards down the hall when he heard a voice call after him. "Tatsuya's father. Excuse me, Tatsuya's father," the voice echoed in the empty halls.

Chemah turned and saw the mother of the child who had beaten up Tatsuya, walking swiftly toward him. Chemah's face did not change expression as she smiled up at him. It was obvious to him what she wanted. *This bitch has no shame*, he thought.

He had used his peripheral vision while talking to Tatsuya and had seen how she had brazenly licked her lips and ogled his ass and back muscles through his clothing, without care of how her son was watched her.

"Hi," she said when she finally reached him. "My name is Anne," she said, holding out her hand for Chemah to shake.

Chemah shook her hand but did not smile down at her as he once might have. She seemed to be waiting for Chemah to say his name.

When an uncomfortable amount of time had passed and he merely stared at her, she pressed on nervously. "I simply wanted to say that I'm sorry about what happened with our kids today. Maybe we could go out for a cup of coffee or something to discuss how we could make sure it doesn't happen again."

The woman was staring up into Chemah's handsome and tanned face. She was looking into his hypnotizing green eyes and almost swooned when his full, moist lips started to speak. Only the words that he spoke were not the words she expected.

"I don't think that'll be necessary, Anne," he said pointedly. "I'm sure you'll talk to your boy and make sure this doesn't happen again."

The woman was taken aback by Chemah's response and was not sure that his assertion was not a veiled threat. "Yes, I'll talk to him," she whispered to Chemah's back as he rushed away. She stared after him, admiring the way his dreadlocks swung loosely down his back. The black Donna Karan suit he wore fit flawlessly over his well-muscled body and she was reminded of a lion as he walked the rest of the way down the hall. As he walked through the doorway and out of her sight, Anne consoled herself. "He must be gay."

‡‡‡

In his element, Chemah did resemble a lion. A lion sniffing out the scent of his prey. He stalked up and down the crime scene, being cautious as to where he stepped to not crush some unseen piece of evidence. He continued to walk for at least an hour when his boss's car pulled up to the yellow police tape that he had ordered around the area.

Chemah watched as the man he referred to only as "sir" struggled with his immense girth to get out of the passenger side of the car. The immense man waited a moment and then gave an impatient wave, indicating that the driver should get out of the car. Chemah had never known his boss to use a driver and was curious as to who he had allowed to act as his chauffeur. Chemah was surprised at the appearance of the man who stepped out of the car. He was as tall as Chemah, and his facial features were sharp like those of a model. He wore his hair in the exact same dreadlocked fashion as Chemah, and wore his facial hair in a Vandyke goatee fashion, like Chemah, as well.

Chemah thought that if the man's skin had not been such a deep shade of brown, he might pass as a younger version of himself. Chemah took a moment to look over the younger man's attire and changed his mind. "You'd never catch me dead in a cheap suit like that," he said to himself, laughing at his own narcissism.

Chemah's boss took slow deliberate steps as he walked toward Chemah. As if he did not want to trip over the smooth cobblestones of the old street or maybe, Chemah thought, as if he were putting off an inevitable but unwanted meeting. Chemah's experience with him suggested that he had certainly never been a man to curb his tongue when he was doing his job.

Chemah felt better, thinking that he simply didn't want to fall on the slippery stone. After all, he was nearing retirement and cops always got real careful with everything around that time. "Anything that can go wrong will go wrong" is what the short-timers always said.

"Hey, Chemah, how's it going? Do we have any leads?" Chemah's boss asked.

"No, sir," Chemah responded, already anticipating the same question he always asked. "This one is covering his tracks very well. He's doing the killing far from here. There are too many tire tracks all over the road to tell which ones might be his. And he apparently is covering his shoes with some sort of plastic to keep from leaving an imprint. From what Kelly is telling me, the way that the footprints are being made by this person's gait, he or she might actually be wearing a shoe that is maybe one, two, or even three sizes too big for him or her."

"You said she?" Chemah's boss asked.

"Yeah, it could be a woman if the size of the foot in the shoe is as small as Kelly thinks it is. The only inconsistency being that if it is a woman she's one strong bi…" Chemah bit his lip from saying the B word.

Ever since he'd had his daughter he'd been trying to refrain from using that word. "One strong girl," Chemah corrected himself. "You see, the prints from the highway to the dumping ground are very clear," Chemah said. "The killer didn't drag the body, he carried it. I don't know why this person didn't simply dump the body out of the car, but he must've had a good reason because he carried her at least fifty yards away from where he stopped his car. The body weighs approximately one hundred and fifty pounds. In order for a woman to carry that much dead weight that far, she'd have to be damn strong."

"Well, keep at it," Chemah's boss said. "We're bound to have missed something."

When his boss didn't say anything else, Chemah turned his attention to the man standing slightly to the right and behind Chemah's boss, looking at the ground as though searching for some kind of clues himself. Chemah looked into his boss's face for a signal and when he got none, nodded toward the stranger.

"Ah yes, Chemah, this is Detective Keith Medlin. Medlin, this is Detective

Chemah Rivers." The younger, darker-skinned version of Chemah stepped forward and extended his hand for Chemah to shake. He had very white teeth and seemed to want to show every one of them as his face broke into an enormous smile. "It's good to meet you, Detective," he said, pumping Chemah's hand vigorously.

"When they told me I would be partnering up with you, I couldn't believe my good luck," Keith exclaimed. "They used two of your cases in the detective training program as case studies, but I looked up most of your other cases myself. I'm sort of a fan of yours."

Chemah could tell the younger man wasn't merely kissing his ass. He sounded genuinely enthusiastic. That fact didn't keep Chemah from being annoyed by this new development. He now understood why his boss had come out of the car so reluctantly. His boss wasn't looking at him. Instead, he looked past Chemah into the waters of the Henry Hudson River. Chemah thought to protest his boss's assignment of this New Jack to work with him. His boss knew that Chemah preferred to work alone as a rule, and Chemah also knew that if his boss had had a choice in the matter, he would be allowed to continue to be a lone ranger. The embarrassment he saw on his boss's face was enough to let him know that this decision was not his. *Everyone has a boss,* Chemah thought. This decision must have come from somewhere else. It would be futile to rant and show his ass over something that he couldn't change anyway, so he chose the higher road.

"Good to have you aboard," he said, shaking Keith's hand back just as enthusiastically.

"Good," Chemah's boss said abruptly as if he had snapped out of a trance. "Chemah, show the kid the ropes. I hear he was pretty smart at the academy, which means he knows dick about the job. Make sure he doesn't fuck anything up." He turned his attention to Keith. "Kid, do whatever he tells you and maybe you'll actually learn something." With that, the boss turned on his heels and started walking toward his car. After ten steps or so he turned around and addressed Keith. "Keys," he said, snapping his fingers at Keith. Keith tossed the boss the car keys he held in his hand and the boss caught them easily. "Get a ride with Chemah," he said and turned, leaving the two dreads to their investigation.

Chemah and Keith turned toward the yellow tape at the same time and started to walk the crime scene again as if it were the most natural thing for them to be doing together. From afar it looked liked two men joined at the hip looking at the ground. "Is he always in such a good mood?" Keith asked, his eyes never leaving the ground."

"Nah, the boss is all right. He's been suffering with yeast infections lately. It's been making him kind of cranky," Chemah answered, with his eyes still glued to the ground in front of him.

"A yeast infection?" Keith said, unbelievingly. "He needs to do something about his immune system, if it's causing that type of attitude, because I ain't checking for that snapping-your-fingers–at-me shit again," Keith said, looking over his shoulder to make sure no one else was within hearing range.

"Make sure you stay healthy and fit if you're going to be with me in a car all day. I got kids at home and can't afford to take any germs home with me," Chemah informed Keith.

"You got kids? Shit, you don't have to worry about me, Chemah," Keith answered back. "I couldn't catch a yeast infection if I fucked two loaves of bread."

Chemah and Keith both stopped and looked at each other at the same time. Both tried to keep looking seriously at the other. Chemah broke into a fit of laughter first and Keith followed. It took them a full two minutes to compose themselves before they could start walking the scene again. Chemah was happy to have a partner and Keith was happy to be a partner.

Chapter 2
SEEING IS BELIEVING

T he gentle dancing of the rain on Michelle's face gave her a feeling of being truly cleansed that the shower she had taken before she left her apartment had not accomplished.

She allowed her dog, Base, to lead her down the street; knowing that he would stop at every corner as he was trained to do.

Her first two seeing-eye dogs had been very good, but she and Base were symbiotic. He had become an extension of her almost from the moment they had started training together. She had chosen him because of the excitement that she had heard in his breathing when she had stopped to pet him. If she had been able to see, she would have known that Base was a mutt. His dark purple tongue hung out loosely the first time Michelle rubbed her hand firmly up and down his throat.

To everyone else that was familiar with dogs, the dark purple tongue was an indicator that Base was at least part Chow, a breed known for its dark disposition. What color is he? she'd asked the trainer who was working with her. "He's jet black," the trainer had said, looking disapprovingly at the dog that he had intended to rid the Service Animal Training Program of permanently. The dog had bitten him yesterday and he had not had the chance to send him off to the ASPCA. "This is the one," Michelle said, smiling up into the empty space in front of her as if someone were taking a picture. "I think you should meet a few other dogs before you make your decision," the trainer had said, anticipating a lawsuit if the dog turned on her like he had done to him. Michelle would not change her mind. She sensed a certain surliness in the dog that she felt was akin to her own.

Now whenever her dog growled at some wayward person who didn't expect that sort of temperament from a service animal, Michelle liked to say, "Just because someone or something doesn't love you the way you want them to, doesn't mean they don't love you with all they have." It was the way she defended her own contempt for other people's feelings and it seemed to work as well for the dog.

It was 5:30 in the morning and it was their regular routine to take a long walk from their apartment on 96th Street all the way up to Grant's Tomb on 122nd Street in Riverside Park. Michelle unconsciously counted how many times they had stopped and knew that they were now on 103rd Street and Broadway.

The smell of coffee coming from the bagel shop on the corner reminded her that she had not eaten since early yesterday afternoon.

Yesterday, when she had expected Karsem to come over around twelve o'clock for their scheduled afternoon of "freelove." That was the term she coined for having sex with a person without the presence of love to create inhibitions.

It had been Michelle's experience in the past that when men fell in love with her they projected a Madonna complex onto her. Something stupid in their minds told them that they couldn't do all the nasty things they used to do to her before they fell in love and their hearts had taken over. She didn't have a problem with the falling-in-love piece. It simply wasn't her thing. She had her career to think about and there wasn't enough of her to give totally to someone else. She knew she would never fall in love.

Before she became a blind woman, she had had aspirations of someday being someone's wife and mother, but now that she knew the harsh reality of being blind, she no longer considered it an option. She could barely take care of herself; she flung away the thought of a helpless child dependent on her for protection from the cold cruel world she herself often sought shelter from. And on the matter of a husband, she wouldn't burden anyone she cared about with her disability.

Michelle believed she was still attractive. Although she couldn't see herself anymore, she remembered how men had stared at her big, full bosom. Genetics had given all of the women in her family big breasts and huge nipples to go with them. When she was younger and not used to the attention they drew, she would try to hide them by wearing big sweaters, but no matter how hard she tried or what bra she wore her huge nipples would show through. Her fair skin, she remembered, never held a blemish. The freckles that dotted her cheeks were a reminder that she should not take too much sun. Her hair had always been long, but nappy as all hell. She remembered begging her mother for her first perm at age fifteen. Since then men had teased her, saying corny things like, "Girl, you must have Indian in your family."

She had never been teased by anyone in her neighborhood. The Thomas family was well known in the Frederick Douglass projects in Brownsville. The original six Thomas brothers had brought their families there and each had at least five children. They were all raised together and taught to have one another's back. If you fucked with one of them, the whole housing project would very likely come down on your head.

When she turned sixteen, Michelle began to notice that women and men alike would turn envious stares at her voluptuous figure as she walked. That was when she started telling jokes. It was the easiest way to keep people from noticing how beautiful she was. She would keep them laughing and eventually they would notice her inner beauty. Her whole family was full of jokes, but she was by far the funniest one of them all.

Michelle's quick wit was as renowned in the projects as her tough cousins' proclivity for violence. During a heated childhood argument with a boy in her building, the boy realized that he could not win the argument and decided to end it with "suck my dick." Even at the age of twelve she had been sharp enough to answer, "What dick? Your dick is so small that when you pee, you wet your own balls. Shit, if you pulled it out right now, you probably wouldn't be able to tell the difference between your thumb and your dick." Later she realized that the boy had liked her and had only been doing what little boys do, that is, anything that will get a girl's attention.

Michelle's full red lips pursed into a smile remembering that young man. Four years later after a movie together, she had let him feel her up in the staircase of the building they both lived in. If someone hadn't come up the stairs in time, she probably would have gotten one of her titties let out into the open air. As she remembered how he had played with her nipples, the doorbell rang.

She felt Base stir as the bell went off for the second time. "I've got it, boy, down, relax," she told Base. Uneasily, Base laid back down on his stomach, but his head stayed up and alert waiting to see who walked into the apartment.

Michelle opened the door without asking who it was. She could tell who her guests were primarily by how they rang her doorbell. To her trained ear, everyone had a distinctive way of ringing it. Karsem White tended to kind of lean on the doorbell as if he were trying to push his way in through that very button. "Hello, Karsem," she said, holding the doorknob with her right hand while her left hand stayed on her hip. "You're running a little late for our appointment, aren't you?" she said, her smile bereft of any good humor. Before he could answer, Michelle's head snapped sharply to her left as if she had caught a glimpse of something out of the corner of her blank eyes. "Who's this?" Michelle said, the fake smile now totally gone from her face. She was staring at a space three inches to the left of the face and smelling a new cologne.

Karsem didn't bother to look in the same direction Michelle's head faced. "This is my man, Ajay," Karsem answered. "I thought after our conversation last week that maybe you'd enjoy some different company," he said.

Michelle's hand left her hip and reached out to her left in search of the face of the man named Ajay. Realizing what she was trying to do, Ajay moved his face slightly to the left so that it would intersect with Michelle's hand as it extended to its full reach. Michelle's outstretched hand first came in contact with his full lips and wide mouth. Her thumb traced a path from his cheekbone, to his ear, and down his jaw line, coming to rest on his chin. She held his chin between her thumb and forefinger and turned back to Karsem. "He's cute enough," she said, the pretend smile coming back to her face. "Both of you come on in."

Michelle released Ajay's face and he stepped forward, prepared to step over the threshold of the doorway. Karsem brushed Ajay backward, using his forearm like a toll arm. He spoke to Michelle but looked at Ajay, who had a confused look on his face. "Did you put that dog away in the other room?" he asked, still holding Ajay at bay.

"Come on in, Base won't bother you," Michelle said.

"You mean Base won't bother you," Karsem corrected her. "Last time I was here he was looking at me like I was a pork chop."

Ajay had not spoken yet, but he took the moment to look over Michelle's shoulder and into the apartment. He saw the dog they were speaking about. He saw Base stir and as their eyes met he was glad that Karsem had stopped him from entering the apartment. The dog seemed to be already sneering at him and it made him take a meaningful step backward away from Karsem's arm. Karsem laughed at him and nodded his agreement at the sentiment he saw in Ajay's eyes. "All right, all right, give me a second, I'll put him in the bathroom," Michelle finally agreed. She took Base by the collar and he allowed her to lead him into the bathroom. As she closed the door on him she could feel herself getting moist between her legs at the thought of what she was about to enjoy with the two men who waited at the door.

Michelle went back to the door and opened it again. This time she didn't say anything, she merely waved in the two waiting men. Karsem came through the door first and Ajay walked close behind him. After a few steps into the apartment, Karsem stopped and waited for Michelle to lead them into the apartment. It was dark except for the light coming through the windows in the other rooms. Michelle locked the door behind them and then turned back toward the two waiting men. They pressed themselves against the left wall, allowing her to pass them and take the lead into the apartment. Michelle passed the two men, allowing her hand to gently scrape against the right wall as a guide into the apartment.

Karsem had been in the apartment at least a dozen times since he and Michelle had met and was no longer impressed with its style. Ajay, on the other hand, was surprised by the setting he was stepping into. Even in the semidarkness, he could see that the place was posh. Karsem had told him all about this wild, blind chick who wanted to get fucked by two guys at the same time, but he had downplayed how beautiful she was, and he definitely had not said anything about the bad crib they were supposed to be going to. *This chick must be rich,* he thought to himself, as he noticed the three original Charles Bibbs paintings hanging side by side on one wall of the dining room through which they were now passing. He saw several other original paintings by other renowned black artists and thought of the irony that a blind woman held these treasures in this dark apartment. Karsem had made him promise not to say a word during the whole time he was to be in the apartment. He had been told that it was one of the stipulations on which the blind woman they were going to have sex with had insisted.

Michelle led them into the living room and unceremoniously plopped herself down on the large, gray mohair couch in the middle of the room. It was the centerpiece of the room and looked like it had cost a fortune. "Make yourselves a drink if you'd like," Michelle said, allowing her arm to fall backward over the couch and point in the general direction of the small bar that was directly behind her at the far wall of the room.

Karsem looked at Ajay, who was about to help himself to the alcohol offered, and nodded no to him. "No thank you," he said to Michelle. Karsem signaled to Ajay to sit on Michelle's right side, as he gently sidled up to the left of her, gently allowing her thigh to come in contact with his own.

Although Karsem had surprised her by bringing along a second person for their "freelove" session, he knew she would be with it. She was the one who had brought up this sexual fantasy the last time they were together. She was also the one who had suggested that the second person involved in this fantasy not have a voice so that it would feel more like she was making love to one person with many appendages, rather than two people. Karsem didn't waste any more time. He knew that he was merely a vessel by which Michelle fulfilled her need for sex and he was fine with that. She was beautiful and all, but she had too many issues for him to be thinking about making her his girl, he had always thought. This was the final act that would clinch the direction their relationship would always go in. He would never again think of getting into a serious relationship with this woman once she took on two men at the same time.

Michelle sat with her hands in her lap, facing forward, when Karsem took her face in both of his hands and turned it forcefully toward him, only to kiss her gently on the mouth. Michelle answered his gentleness by allowing her lips to part ever so slightly so that her tongue could dart out to lick his upper lip. His lip felt soft and full, tasting of the orange juice he must have drunk before coming to her apartment. It made her want to taste his bottom lip, so she allowed her tongue to trace along the outer edges of his mouth until she could taste the same sweetness on this much thicker bottom lip. Her tongue had already memorized the most savory part of Karsem's mouth from their previous exploits and searched for it as Karsem allowed her full access into his mouth. Michelle found his tongue and sucked it into her mouth. She let it slip in and out in imitation of an act she planned on performing on his penis after she finished with his mouth. Not one to be ignored, Ajay leaned against Michelle's back, allowing her to feel the swell of his own massive chest against her back.

Michelle felt the body of the man behind her and from its hardness knew that he was in shape. Ajay lifted the hair that hung down about Michelle's shoulders and kissed at the nape of her neck. Michelle's breath began to come in short hard gasps as she continued to suck Karsem's tongue. She felt her blouse fall about her shoulders as Ajay reached around in front of her and undid the final button at her throat. As it fell, Ajay dragged it the rest of the way off one arm, then the other. He tossed the blouse over the side of the sofa and before he could think of what to do next, he felt Michelle's hand reach deftly for his half-open zipper and jam her hand into it to grab hold of his hardening penis. Not satisfied with feeling it through his underwear, she attempted to reach over the elastic but instead found the spongy head of his penis where she thought the elastic would be. She lingered with Karsem's tongue for another moment and then made the decision to turn around and focus her attention on getting Ajay's pants off.

As she turned around on her knees and started fumbling with Ajay's belt, Karsem took the opportunity to reach around her and undo the button of her pants. Michelle found her pants being tugged off her hips as she was simultaneously tugging the pants off Ajay's hips. Neither she nor Karsem would stop working on their self-appointed assignments to allow the other an advantage in finishing first. Ajay looked amused as he watched the two struggle. As Michelle got the pants around his ankles, Ajay decided to take care of the underwear himself. He raised his hips off the couch and pushed the boxers down to his ankles where Michelle was getting the jeans off his feet. Michelle felt the underwear touch her hands and ripped them the rest of the way off him in one swift movement. She wasn't wasting any more time. She could already feel the wetness dripping down the inner part of her thigh.

Michelle used both her hands to guide her up the length of Ajay's thighs until her head banged against his six-pack abs. Michelle then lowered her face until her lips were touching the spongy head of his dick. Michelle let go of Ajay's thighs and grabbed his dick at the base with two hands, much the same way you would hold a baseball bat. She knew it would be huge, because she had told Karsem that she preferred men with big penises. She took a deep breath through her nose and let the full weight of her head fall onto the huge penis until the head hit the back of her throat. She didn't use any up-and-down movement, she simply sucked at the base with her lips and tongue and continued to force more and more of his penis into her gullet.

While Michelle got her professional on, Karsem was busy licking the trail of vaginal juices from her right inner thigh all the way up to her cunny. When he reached the opening that was the origin of the rich-tasting juices he was enjoying, he licked a last dangling drop from her opening before leaning back to admire the thick lips that were hanging open in welcome. He had been with Michelle enough times to know not to dally too long with the oral sex. He enjoyed licking her and she had said she enjoyed it to a certain extent, but she mostly wanted it hard and fast.

Ajay watched Michelle's hand reach underneath the cushion of the couch they were on, and after a moment came up with a Magnum condom without once letting up on the suctioning she was giving him. The package appeared to already be partially opened so that Michelle had only to pull the condom out, without the struggle of ripping the package open. It meant she was prepared, Ajay thought.

When she got the condom out of the wrapper, she wasted no time in extricating the massive penis from her throat. It was the color of deep dark chocolate and it glistened with the saliva that painted every inch of it. Ajay was very proud of his cock and was disappointed that Michelle could not stare at it in awe as some of his other lovers had.

When Karsem saw the condom in Michelle's hand he panicked. He did not think things would progress this rapidly. He didn't have his condom ready. Nor did he have the lubrication out that he knew he would need. Karsem jumped off the couch and started to rip his own clothing off. He watched in fascinated horror as Michelle carefully pulled the condom down Ajay's long shaft and made no great show of clambering over his legs before settling over the massive head she had sucked on.

Michelle let her ass fall into Ajay's lap as her head snapped back and her mouth fell open in a silent scream. Michelle was riding Ajay's rigid shaft for a full thirty seconds before she felt Karsem behind her again. She felt a cold wetness flow down the crack of her ass and knew what he was preparing her for. She was no stranger to anal sex. She enjoyed rough sex, and there was nothing rougher than this, she thought. The problem was she was so full of cock already and she didn't know if her body could stand another ounce of it. She had never been with two men, but she had decided that she would not deprive herself of experiences in this life that her blindness didn't hinder her from. There were already too many things that she would not be able to do because of her blindness.

Michelle felt Karsem's fingers massage the lubricant into her ass. One finger slipping in and out of her and then two. The different sensations coming from her ass, then her pussy were about to drive her insane. Michelle felt Karsem pull his fingers out of her and immediately felt a greater pressure on her backside created by the blunt head of his dick. Michelle tried to concentrate on the penis in her vagina that was causing her such delight, but the pressure on her ass was becoming ridiculous. She could feel drops of Karsem's sweat falling on her back and thought the restraint he was using to keep from ramming himself into her in one stroke was to be commended.

When Karsem's dickhead slipped through her sphincter Michelle could swear lights went off in her head. Karsem paused for a moment and she breathed a sigh of relief. Karsem took that sigh as permission to push the rest of his length into her outstretched rear opening. "Aaaiiiiieeeeeeeeeeee…" Michelle wailed into the afternoon air as the oxygen rushed out of her lungs. Karsem didn't stop stroking into her. He was already used to the screams.

‡‡‡

As Michelle remembered the scenarios she had experienced throughout yesterday afternoon and into the night, she winced at the phantom pleasure-pain she felt between her legs.

"Aiieeee…" Michelle heard a high-pitched but muffled scream that brought her out of her own reverie. The scream was one of pain, she thought, remembering her own anguish yesterday afternoon. Michelle knew the park was mostly desolate at this time of the day. It was the only reason that she came out at this early hour.

Base continued to lead Michelle along Riverside Park. He led her another ten paces when she heard a muffled whimpering sound and stopped in her tracks. Michelle attempted to detect which direction the crying was coming from when she heard a man's voice coming from where she thought the crying emanated. She tried to listen closer.

"We're almost finished now." The man's voice was heavy with emotion. He also seemed to be breathing hard. Michelle could tell the voices were coming from either the back of a truck or a van from the way the voice she was listening to was echoing. There had to be a lot of metallic space for it to bounce off that way. "Let's pray together now," he said. Michelle took a step closer to the voice before Base tugged back on his harness, indicating that she was moving too close to the street. Michelle stopped again and listened to the man's prayer. "Lord, release this woman from her misery," *thwack, mmmmph*. Michelle heard the sickening sounds of metal crushing bone and flesh and a woman struggling in great pain. She started to walk quickly away from the voices, but couldn't do so quickly enough to keep from hearing the man's prayer: "Lose the demons from this whore's body." *Kthunk. Eeeiiiii.* ...With each strike there was less of a struggle.

Michelle wanted to run, but was so afraid of falling that she urged Base on with a shake of the harness. The jingling metal of the harness had been too loud, she feared, and she doubled her steps. Michelle continued on through the park, afraid to call the police for fear that whoever it was that was hurting that woman would hear her before she could find an officer. Michelle thought the best thing to do was get out of the park as fast as she could and call the police when she got home.

Michelle didn't know where she was anymore. She knew that if she made a right off the next sidewalk and walked straight for two blocks she would be on Broadway again. She would feel safer there, she thought. At least she would hear cars passing again. When she got to Broadway she made another right and Base seemed to know they were on their way back home. Michelle loosened her grip on the harness and allowed Base to find his way home. She wouldn't feel safe until she reached the sanctity of her apartment. The cold sweat that trickled down her spine urged her to move faster. She had the uneasy feeling that she was being followed, but didn't dare stop. What good would that do? she asked herself.

As she walked block after block, she sensed more and more people on the street around her. People had started coming out to go to work. A few people walked by her and close enough next to her that she could smell their particular body odors. She was scared, but she had enough sense of self-preservation that she was waiting for, and anticipating, the metallic smell and taste of blood that had overcome her, as she had listened to the woman being beaten in the vehicle.

If the man who had been in that car was following her and came close enough she would not be caught unprepared. She had her left hand in the pocket of her hoody, firmly rapped around the box cutter she always carried with her. It was open all the way, and she wouldn't be afraid to use it. When she had first found out that she was going blind, she had promised herself that she would never be anyone's victim. The box cutter was nothing new. Every girl in her neighborhood had carried one from the time they turned thirteen. Although she had never had opportunity to use it, she knew that it would not be an issue for her.

Michelle knew that she was now two blocks from her apartment, as she felt the swirl of air come up from the subway station she was now passing. She wanted to wipe the sweat from her forehead, but would have to let go of her box cutter to do it. She opted to let the sweat run its course. When she was a few yards from her building, she had the terrible urge to run the rest of the way. She stopped the panic in her head by reciting her old neighborhood's credo: Brownsville's down, always chill, never ran, never will. The saying gave Michelle her old bravado back and she was able to let go of her box cutter and grab hold of her keys as she came to her building door. As she pressed the key into the lock, she felt Base's head whip around, almost resting the harness from her grasp. He snarled once and barked loudly. Michelle quickly thrust her hand back into her hoody jacket and grasped the box cutter. She pulled it out and held it behind her back to shield it from anyone that was in front of her. She knew that she had the door at her back and was not worried that someone would come from behind.

Moments seemed to turn into hours as she waited shakily for the attack to come, but none did. After about five seconds she couldn't wait any longer. She sniffed the air hard, but couldn't catch a whiff of what she was dreading. Michelle tried to tell herself it was her imagination, but knew right on the surface that she was deluding herself. Base had smelled it, even though she couldn't. She had led the villain right to her apartment building. It was a stupid move, and one she couldn't take back. It couldn't be helped now, but she wouldn't allow her pride to let her keep making mistakes. She would not enter the building on her own. She would wait right here for someone she knew to come in or out and escort her to her apartment.

Base had relaxed. She didn't believe she was in any more danger, but she was not letting go of her blade. She waited by the door as stiff and stolid as a wooden soldier. Ten minutes passed before the door creaked open. "Good morning, Michelle," came the voice of her upstairs neighbor.

"Good morning, Mr. Cochrane," Michelle said, finally relieved to hear the voice of someone familiar. "Can I trouble you to escort a tired, young woman to her apartment?" Michelle asked.

"Is something wrong?" Mr. Cochrane asked, his eyes darting from left to right, looking around for some sign of danger.

"No, I'm a little tired," Michelle lied. "I've sort of lost my bearings, if you know what I mean," she said, finally letting go of the box cutter to wipe her brow.

"No problem," Mr. Cochrane said, reaching out in an attempt to take Michelle by the elbow.

He snatched his hand back just in time as Base lunged straight at him. Michelle had felt the dog rush and had also pulled Base back quickly.

"I'm sorry, Mr. Cochrane. You know Base, he's simply being overprotective."

Mr. Cochrane's good nature allowed him to laugh off the attack. It wasn't the first time he had gotten too close to Michelle. He turned around, still laughing, and used his keys to open the door.

"Hey, Michelle, I still remember what you said to me the last time Base took a piece out of me," he said good-naturedly. "Just because someone doesn't love you the way you want them to, doesn't mean they don't love you with all they have." Michelle could almost appreciate Mr. Cochrane's humor, but she was still worried about what Base had sensed and she hadn't. Only one thing was for sure: she would never return to that park again.

Chapter 3

IN THE NAME OF THE FATHER

After putting his money in the collection plate, Victor Brown bowed his head and prayed. He knew he had a lot to atone for now. This time that he was putting into the church was but a small price that he owed to the Lord. He barely heard the sermon that the preacher was screaming from the pulpit as he prayed about the news headlines in this morning's paper.

Yesterday another woman had been found bludgeoned to death on the side of the Henry Hudson Parkway. The victim had been wrapped in tape from head to toe and covered with a blanket. Victor prayed for the victim over and over again. Prayed that she had made peace with the Lord before she died, and prayed that the person who did this would be caught soon.

By the time he raised his head, Victor found that the congregation was filing out of the church. Mrs. Brown was in the middle of the throng of churchgoers walking around outside, passing on a good word to those who needed one and admonishing those she felt were not being humble in the eyes of the Lord. Mrs. Brown was once the most beautiful woman in the entire church; in the whole damn neighborhood, if you ever heard the elder deacons talking about her in hushed whispers during a church outing, where they were able to let go of some of the holy ways that their wives had imposed upon them.

It was already sundown as Mrs. Brown looked up to admire the full moon that filled the sky. She seemed in an especially good mood when Victor came down the stairs of the church.

The younger women that surrounded Mrs. Brown at the foot of the church steps smiled coyly and bid a quick good-bye to Victor before dispersing. They had all been the victim of Mrs. Brown's tongue at one point or another and did not want to be accused of trying to flirt with the love of her life. Mrs. Brown kissed Victor on his cheek and put her arm through his as she waved good-bye to the last few parishioners and she and Victor walked off toward their apartment. Mrs. Brown didn't know why Victor was in such bad humor lately, but she knew better than to ask the reason. Victor had always been close-mouthed about his feelings, sharing little more than his daily activities.

"I have a special dinner waiting for you at home, baby," she whispered in his ear. Victor was immediately alert. He knew what a special dinner meant. It always went with a special dessert.

The walk to their apartment was interspersed with talk of the preacher's message this evening and some of the gossip that Mrs. Brown had gleaned from some of her closer cohorts. "And Ms. Jenkins had no business wearing such a low neckline like that, sitting all up in the front pew like nobody knows she trying to get Pastor's attention. She ain't foolin' nobody." Victor tried to ignore this last remark as he tried not to think badly of anybody, especially those in his church. He had a knack for being unforgiving once he thought someone had sinned in the eyes of the Lord. Victor discarded the thought from his mind and wiped his feet on the welcome mat in front of his door before turning the key and letting in the lady of the house.

"Take your coat right off and come sit at the table. It'll only take me a minute to heat up this chicken and dumplings," Mrs. Brown said, taking her own coat off and placing it around the back of a kitchen chair. The Southern meal took three minutes to heat up, but Victor could smell the goodness coming from the microwave oven after two minutes of sitting at the kitchen table. While they were waiting for the food to heat, Mrs. Brown came behind his chair and started messing in his short Afro. She feigned picking a piece of lint out of it and then commenced massaging his scalp. She knew something was bothering him and she aimed to relieve as much of his stress as she could. Her hands went from his scalp down to his shoulders, and after a few moments she could not keep her hands from roaming down to his tight wiry chest. She massaged his pectoral muscles more for her pleasure than his. The microwave timer went off as if on cue for her to stop. She knew that any physical display of affection outside of the bedroom made Victor nervous.

Mrs. Brown pulled the plate out of the microwave and placed it in front of Victor, making him back away from the steam that was generated from the plate.

"Is it too hot?" she asked him, a frown coming to her face. Victor shook his head no.

"Thank you, this is fine," Victor said, picking up his fork and shoveling a mound of rice and a piping-hot dumpling into his mouth. The food burned his mouth and he made an oval of his lips and blew out puffs of air as if he were in a Lamaze class, practicing his breathing for a birth.

Mrs. Brown sat across from him while he ate.

"Aren't you going to eat?" Victor asked her.

"No, baby, I'm simply going to sit here and wait for you to finish so that I can give you your dessert. I know you've been thinking about it since we left the church."

Victor put his head down and put another forkful in his mouth, ashamed that Mrs. Brown knew his thoughts so well. Ten minutes later, Victor was putting the last bite of gravy-soaked chicken into his mouth and chewing, it slowly as he pushed the plate away from the edge of the table. He rubbed his belly to indicate that he was full and satisfied.

The gesture brought a smile to Mrs. Brown's mouth as she picked up the plate and took it to the sink.

"You must be tired, baby," she said to Victor. "Why don't you go into the bedroom and take off your clothes. After I clean up some here, I'll be in to give you a nice massage before you go to bed." Victor got up slowly. Not wanting to look too anxious to get his dessert, he loped slowly to the bedroom, dragging his feet the whole way as if exhausted. When he reached the bedroom door he turned the doorknob and pushed it open, not surprised to see an exact image of himself reflected in the mirror across the room. Victor walked toward the mirror and stood directly in front of it as he undid the knot in his tie. He carefully folded the tie, then after a second, thought better of it and flung it onto the floor of the closet to his right. He was not in a carefree mood tonight and this bothered him. He did not like feeling controlled and had thrown his tie as a sign of defiance. Weak as this symbolic gesture was, it made him feel better.

Victor watched himself in the mirror as he loosened each button of his shirt. With each button unfastened, he felt more and more anxious at the prospect of what was to come. His fingers trembled as the button on his left cuff stuck in its hole. He shook his left arm inside of the sleeve and tried to calm his nerves. His second attempt at the cuff was successful and he had no problem at all with the right. Victor shrugged the shirt off his shoulders and pulled it off, launching it in the same direction as his tie.

Victor looked down at his feet, which appeared too small for his body, and kicked off his shoes, sending them under the bed. He started to undo his belt and changed his mind instead pulling off the wife beater T-shirt he'd had under his shirt. He allowed the T-shirt to fall to his side, thinking he'd have to put it back on after his dessert. He stared in the mirror at the curly hair covering his chest. Ashamed at the need to touch his own nipples, he quickly put his hands to other use by taking off the remainder of his belt and unbuttoning his slacks. He allowed the pants to drop, puddling around his ankles, and then used each foot to help the other pull away from the clinging pants. All that was left were his socks and underwear.

As he looked at himself in the mirror again, he could not help but allow his hands to roam over his tight chest, allowing his palms to come to rest over his hardening nipples. He closed his eyes and felt his breath quicken as his hands slid down his torso and into the elastic band of his underwear. Victor cupped his hands under his huge balls and allowed himself to feel the weight of them when he was startled out of his ecstasy by the sensuous whisper of a voice behind him. "Let me do that for you, baby," she said. Before Victor could yank his hands out of his underwear in embarrassment, he felt two smaller, softer hands come under the elastic, covering his hands and keeping him from releasing his own genitals. "Mmmmmm, they feel full," the voice whispered into his ear.

Victor could feel Mrs. Brown's soft, full tits pressed against his back. She must have taken her clothes off in the kitchen, he thought, as her small pebble-like nipples stung into his back. He knew the wet feeling rolling down the crack of his ass was from the milk leaking from her breasts. She always expressed milk when she was excited. "As long as you keep sucking them, they'll always feed you," she had once told him. Mrs. Brown didn't look bad for a forty-two-year-old woman. Her breasts sagged only slightly. She didn't eat all of the food that she cooked so her waist was kept at a modest twenty-eight inches and she had an ass you could sit your drink on.

Victor looked into the eyes of the woman who was looking over his shoulder and into the mirror they shared and thought they were the most beautiful almond-colored eyes he'd ever seen. Looking at their faces side by side the way they were, you'd never guess they were twenty-two years apart in age. Mrs. Brown kissed him on the shoulder, then began trailing a wet kiss down his back, licking up the traces of her own milk along the way. She let the weight of her arms drag Victor's underwear down his hips and over his thick thighs. Once they were past, they fell easily to the floor without any further assistance from her.

At this point, her face was parallel to his smooth brown ass. Mrs. Brown could smell the clean but pungent odor that comes from a well-groomed man's body after a long day. She had purposely not told him to bathe first because she liked the musk that permeated from him mingling with her own sweat. She allowed her pert lips to graze the crack of his ass as she breathed in his essence. She breathed deeply, then raised herself back up to her full height.

Their eyes met in the mirror again as she looked over his shoulder and brought her hands around his waist again to settle on his penis. It was already thick and heavy in her hand, but she could feel it lengthen even more as she stroked it. Victor tried to look away, but Mrs. Brown's eyes locked into his and would not let go. She squeezed and pulled on his rock-hard dick, intent on making sure that every ounce of blood it could take filled this vessel of man meat she held in her hands.

Victor breathed through clenched teeth as he felt a drop of his own milk squeeze through the tip of his fat dickhead. A whimper came and then died on his lips when Mrs. Brown, spotting the lubrication in the mirror, inched her right hand up, enabling her to use her thumb to smear the gob of precum up and down the large opening on the head of his dick. She didn't miss a stroke with her other hand and the dual sensations made his head spin. He attempted to move toward the bed, but Mrs. Brown was holding him in place by his dick and he felt she would tear it off by the root if he moved any farther.

She began to lick at his earlobe while she whispered, "Give it to me, baby. Give Momma that milk. Don't hold it back anymore. Give it to me, give it to me, give it to me, give it to me," she chanted in his ear. Victor looked at himself in the mirror and, as if in an outer body experience, witnessed his body starting to tremble uncontrollably. He looked to his right shoulder and into a pair of eyes he would have described as angelic three hours ago at church, but now he saw a fury and madness in the woman that bordered on deranged. Sadly, when he looked back into his own eyes, he saw the same chaotic look.

Unable or unwilling to take control of his own body, he allowed Mrs. Brown to possess him. His penis twitched in her hands and he stiffened and curled his toes as she pointed it directly at the mirror in front of them. The fluid released from his body sprayed into their reflections and slid sickeningly down the mirror. Victor watched in fascination as Mrs. Brown continued to milk the last vestiges of his seed from his body. A glimmer of spittle hung from her slack jaw and she was savagely squeezing his penis when the weight of his body gave way and he started to slump toward the bed next to him. Mrs. Brown expertly guided his body across the bed and allowed her own weight to rest on top of him.

As he looked into his mother's eyes, Victor wondered how many times she had lain this very same way with his father. His mother had told him many times that he was the spitting image of the man, but there were no pictures to attest to it.

Mrs. Brown looked down at her own son and admired the features of the first and only man she had ever loved. He had left her and her two children more than twenty years ago, but she still felt the pain like it was yesterday. Five years ago, she had thrown off to her drunken inhibitions and taken advantage of her own son. She hadn't taken a man since her one and only left her and it had driven her mad.

Reesey Brown and her two children worked the grocery store that was left to her by her father. Everyone in the neighborhood loved her for her grace and good humor. In the years that had passed, many men had attempted to court her. The allure of such a beautiful woman all alone with small children and a thriving business brought many suitors. Reesey had rejected every one of their advances and doted on her two boys.

This is the only man I have left in my life, she thought, as she looked down at Victor. She had no intention of driving this one away, she rationalized.

Reesey Brown felt the stiffness of her son beneath her and history had taught her that he would not go soft until he came at least one more time. She didn't enjoy doing these things, she lied to herself as she felt her vulva opening in invitation to his now brick-like penis. *It's a matter of keeping the family together.* As she slid down onto him she deserted the prayers she had canted to the Lord earlier and submitted to her needs. Mother and son were joined in an unholy union and were bound for life.

Chapter 4
SNITCHES GET STITCHES

hree days after her experience in the park Michelle still hadn't left the sanctity of her apartment. She had blown off a gig she had been looking forward to at Caroline's Comedy Club, deciding that it was best to be easy for a while. On her third day as a shut-in, the guilt of being a coward became too much for her. Her daddy didn't raise any punks. And she sure as hell wouldn't have locked herself away if she'd still had her sight. It took listening via the TV to the gruesome details of another young woman's body being found on Michelle's fourth day indoors for her to act. When she picked up the receiver to dial 911, her hand shook with panic. *What if the killer finds out I was talking to the police?* she thought. "He already knows where I live," she began talking to herself in harsh whispers. "FUUUUUUCK!" Michelle screamed when she finally realized that she had no other choice but to call the police, if for no other reason than for her own protection.

Her hand shook until she dialed the final digit of the police emergency number, but was calmed by the steady voice of the operator.

"Police emergency. How can I help you?" the operator's voice came through clearly.

Michelle steadied her hand on the phone by placing one hand over the other. "Yes, I believe I have some information pertaining to the killings of the young women," Michelle said, her voice cracking in discomfort.

"Hold one second," the operator said. "I'll put you through to the detective in charge of that investigation."

Michelle held for at least thirty seconds, and she had almost decided to hang up the phone, when a man's voice came through the receiver.

"Detective Rivers speaking, how can I help you?" the voice said.

Michelle came closer to hanging up the phone when she heard the voice on the other end. It had scared her, it was so much like her father's. It had passion in it and conviction of authority. She immediately knew the type of man she was speaking to and was not so much in the mood to be admonished or looked down upon by a disapproving stranger. Her father and she were on the outs with each other, and even without knowing this person on the phone, she sensed she was talking to a replica of the patriarch of her own family.

"Never mind, I have the wrong number." Michelle pressed the button that she knew said "End," hanging up the phone.

She stood holding the phone to her chest, wondering what she would do next, when her phone rang, vibrating in her hands, making her fumble it like a badly hit runningback. She gained control of the phone, but had no intention of answering it. She hadn't answered it in days and couldn't think of a reason to now. The phone stopped ringing and she settled down on her sofa to continue listening to the news show she had turned on earlier. A minute passed and her phone rang and vibrated in her hands again. The phone rang eight times, she counted, before the person on the other end hung up the phone, thereby not allowing the answering machine to be activated. This phone activity was repeated for fifteen minutes before Michelle started to feel angry. Five minutes after that, she was ready to fuck somebody up.

She finally answered the phone, hoping it was someone who deserved her wrath. Michelle pressed the button marked "start" and barked into the receiver. "Who the fuck is this?" she asked.

"Hello, Ms. Thomas? This is Detective Chemah Rivers. You called the emergency line some time ago, saying that you had some information about the young women being murdered."

Michelle remained silent, not knowing why the same voice she had heard thirty minutes earlier now made her feel safe instead of angry. "I really don't know how much I can tell you, Detective Rivers. The whole thing is really sketchy to me, I'm not really sure how much I know."

Chemah's voice was even gentler and more patient when he said, "Anything you think you might know could be of some help to us, Ms. Thomas. Whatever you tell us would be in the strictest of confidence."

Michelle allowed a moment of silence to gather after his words before she spoke. "I think I can identify the killer's voice," Michelle blurted into the phone before she could throw off the seductive effect of Chemah's voice.

There was another brief silence on the phone, and this time the silence had an electric feel to it. When Chemah's voice came through the speaker again, Michelle found that it still had a seductive quality to it, but it also contained a strange strain. Michelle was reminded of a good lover holding back his ejaculation so that she could get off first.

"Ms. Thomas, I have your address. Do you mind if I send a car over for you so that we can talk in person?" Chemah gently coaxed her.

Michelle hardened herself to tell this seductive man that she was not leaving the house, but what came out was "Yes, Detective Rivers. Tell the officers to ring Four-F when they get to the building." For good measure she added, "Is the address you have 2561 Broadway?"

"Yes, that's what we have," Chemah answered back.

"I'll be waiting," Michelle said, and waited a few moments to hear if Chemah's soothing voice would offer any further comfort before she pressed the "end" button on her phone again.

Michelle was waiting for five minutes on her couch for the police to arrive before she thought she ought to fix herself up a bit before being escorted to the police station. She had been wearing the same outfit for the second day in a row, she remembered, and had not bothered to bathe this morning. When she finally decided to get up from the couch and do something about her appearance, her door buzzer rang. She answered the buzzer and the police identified themselves before she rang the buzzer to let them up. *So much for changing,* she thought. She briefly remembered Detective Rivers's voice, but was stronger in her own thoughts now that he was not directly in her ear.

Michelle didn't bother going into her room to change. Instead, she went directly to her closet to get her jacket and the harness for Base. *He's probably as old and mean as my father anyway,* she thought, remembering the first impression she'd had of his voice. There was a knock at her door and she called Base to her. Michelle felt Base had been mad at her because she'd made him use the bathroom indoors against his training. She sensed him by her side almost immediately and knew he'd already forgiven her. *This is the only unconditional love I'll ever experience,* she thought.

‡‡‡

At the police precinct, Michelle was led directly into an interview room. Base would not be allowed into the room and Michelle was asked to tether him to the bench that was positioned approximately fifteen feet to the right of the desk sergeant. Chemah and Keith were at their conjoined desks going over the physical evidence they had uncovered at the crime scene when one of the officers who had brought Michelle in came to inform them that their "witness" had arrived. The officer had such a smirk on his face when he spoke that Chemah was bound to ask him what the problem was.

The officer did not want to get on Chemah's bad side and became completely somber when Chemah directly asked him, "Is there a problem, Officer?"

"No problem, sir," the rookie cop answered. The young cop turned to leave but thought twice and turned back to Chemah.

"Sir, you do know that the lady you sent us to get is blind?"

Chemah looked at the young officer as if he had two heads, then he looked back at Keith to make sure that Keith had heard him say the same thing. The look on Keith's face was just as disbelieving as Chemah felt his might be, so he asked the obvious question.

"Officer, did you say that the witness we sent you to get is blind?" Chemah asked, getting up so close to the young officer that he could see the sweat starting to form on the younger man's upper lip.

Instead of answering, the rookie nodded his head up and down. Chemah didn't know what to make of this new information, but thought it best to talk it over with his boss before going into the interview room. Chemah nodded at Keith, signaling him to follow him. After taking a few steps he stopped suddenly to call to the young cop who had brought him his new witness: "What room did you put her in?"

"Room two," the rookie responded, looking a bit more like a grown man than when Chemah was up close to him.

"Thanks, Officer. You did a good job," Chemah praised him before turning to walk away again.

The rookie had a big smile on his face as he walked away. He'd heard a lot about Detective Rivers and was happy that he'd had a chance to meet him. Later on at the bar, he would brag to his friends that he and Chemah had worked on a case that day. No one would believe him and he wouldn't care.

✠✠✠

Chemah walked into his boss's office without knocking and was opening his mouth to talk until he noticed that Keith was not at his side. Chemah turned around to look for Keith and saw him standing outside the threshold of the captain's office. Chemah waved for him to come in, but Keith did not. He seemed to be waiting for permission from the captain. The captain looked up from his work and appeared bored by the detectives who were disturbing him.

"Leave him out there, if he's too fucking scared to come in," the captain said when he realized that Chemah was trying to coax Keith into coming into the office.

Keith heard the captain's insult and stepped into the office to stand by Chemah. He wasn't scared, he thought, nor was he ashamed of himself for not following Chemah's direction. He was simply used to knocking and waiting to be told to come in. That was the protocol the captain at his last command insisted anyone who wanted an audience with him abide by. Now, he stood next to Chemah and let him explain their new dilemma to the captain.

After listening a moment, the captain responded, "So she's blind, but she's said that she could identify the killer."

"She told me on the phone that she could identify his voice," Chemah corrected him. "As soon as she said it I stopped asking questions and had a car pick her up. I didn't think anything of it at the time. It didn't occur to me why she would only be able to identify his voice."

The captain looked thoughtful for a minute and then responded. "Chemah, this is your show. I don't have to tell you how many people are on my ass about these killings. Do what you always do; just do it quicker this time. They've got my balls in a noose over this shit." Then the captain glanced over at Keith with mild contempt. "When you go into the room, let Chemah introduce you, but don't you say a fucking word. You might have gotten in this unit through somebody you know, but right now you're at the top of my shit list. Listen and learn. That's all you're here to do right now, got it?"

Keith didn't bother opening his mouth to reply. He simply nodded his head; acknowledging that he understood. At that point, Chemah's and the captain's eyes locked into each other's. In the brief moment that they held each other's stare they seemed to communicate something that Keith did not understand. Whatever it was, Keith noticed that the captain's shoulders didn't seem as high up on his neck as when he and Chemah had first entered. Chemah and the captain shared a history that Keith would never understand. They had seen a lot of dead bodies together and had shared each other's pain on several occasions. The rookie wouldn't know their connection until he went through some shit of his own. "Let's go," Chemah said to Keith as Batman might have said to Robin.

‡‡‡

Chemah entered the interview room first and Keith came in on his heels. Michelle was sitting at a table facing the door. The other uniformed officer who had brought her in was standing by the window, waiting to be relieved. Chemah came toward the officer and patted him on the back as they passed each other.

"Thanks, Carl," he said to the officer, who only smiled and tipped his hat at Chemah's recognition of him. Keith held the door open for the officer to leave and then closed it quickly, as if trying to keep prying eyes out.

Chemah pulled a chair out on the opposite side of the table to where Michelle was sitting and sat down. At the sound of the chair scraping on the floor, Michelle sat up stiffly. "Ms. Thomas, my name is Detective Chemah Rivers and this is my partner Detective Keith Medlin." Keith held up his hand in greeting and then put it down, stupidly realizing that she could not see him. "Hi," he said awkwardly after a moment. A sharp glance from Chemah reminded Keith that he'd better not say another word until Chemah gave the okay.

Chemah looked at the beautiful young woman in front of him and by the way she turned her ear slightly toward him, as if looking at him through it, he immediately knew that she hadn't been blind her whole life. That would be helpful, he thought. If her memory were any good, she'd be able to describe things that a person who had been blind his or her whole life would not. "Ms. Thomas, would you please tell us what you think you might know about the murders?"

Michelle listened to the voice that she'd heard on the phone and decided that it did have a powerful timbre to it like her father's, but also it had a gentle and seductive quality that her father's did not. She imagined that Chemah was a bit older than her, but not by much. His voice had a sophisticated quality that held no arrogance. Michelle was no longer afraid since she had been in the company of the police officers. Her false bravado came back into her voice. She told the story of what she had experienced in the park four days earlier, almost making herself seem like a heroine in the telling. She told of how she thought she was followed back to her apartment building and embellished how she would have fended off the phantom attacker who had never appeared.

Chemah listened to Michelle's story intently, all the while holding back his questions for fear he would interfere with her train of thought and cause her to skip some important part. He saw the looks on Keith's face as Michelle was talking and was glad that the captain had warned him to keep his mouth shut during the interview. Keith's instincts were good, Chemah thought, as he saw by Keith's face at different times that he wanted to ask questions that Michelle's story did not adequately answer.

As Chemah focused his attention deeper on the woman in front of him, he became enthralled by her beauty. Chemah wasn't normally taken in by beautiful women, but this woman seemed to be oblivious to her own beauty. She wasn't putting on any airs as he thought most beautiful women did. Caught up in his own fantasy, he began to shamelessly watch Michelle's mouth form words that he now found to be erotic, with lips that were full and sensuous and hypnotic. Chemah appeared to be reading her lips and caught the inappropriateness of his own behavior as he almost licked his own lips at the same time she was licking hers.

As she came to the end of her story, he sat up a little more erect. He felt a slight swelling in his pants and thought of the questions he would have to ask to give himself time to lose the hardness he had developed. It would not do to have Keith know what was actually going through his mind.

The three years I've gone without sex are taking their toll on me, he thought. In the past three years whenever he felt the sexual tension build in him to the point that he had to take matters into his own hands, he had alternately used memories of things he had done with his son's mother and, depending on his mood on some days, he'd also remember things he'd done with his daughter's mother. Neither relationship had ended well, but the sex he'd had with each woman was more than adequate to facilitate his masturbation. He knew that tonight as he held his swollen dick in his hand he would remember the sight of Michelle's mouth forming simple vowels and that alone would cause him to waste his seed over his own hand.

Chemah asked the obvious question first.

"How do you know you could identify this voice if you heard it again?" Chemah asked, already knowing the answer.

"I'm blind, Detective Rivers, that's what I do. I remember sounds. You'd be surprised how many distinctive sounds you find around you when you're forced to listen hard," she said, smiling at the memory of the voice of this man she was now speaking directly to.

Chemah pushed on with more questions, and Keith continued to look on, almost about to burst for not being able to ask questions of his own.

After two hours of questions and answers, Keith, who had stood for the whole process, moved to open the door and Chemah reluctantly got up from his seat and thanked Michelle for her time. He prefaced his thank you by acknowledging that they did not have a suspect at this time, but would like her to come down and identify the voice of any suspect they might have in the future.

"I'd be glad to *go down* any time you want me to, Detective Rivers," Michelle replied without skipping a beat. Chemah chose to ignore the simple grammatical error that Michelle made, chalking it up to fatigue. Keith, on the other hand, was not so oblivious to what was on the blind woman's mind and showed it in a lecherous and knowing grin.

Chemah helped Michelle up from her chair and began to escort her out into the main corridor.

"We'll get your pooch and then we'll get you a ride home," Chemah said as he walked her toward the dog he'd seen tethered to the bench when he was walking to the interview room.

Michelle could hear Base's heavy panting as they got close to him.

"Here, let me get him for you," Chemah said, reaching forward to get Base's leash from around the bench.

Before Michelle could warn Chemah, Base had already lunged for his arm with his canine teeth bared. Chemah caught the dog in midair by the throat and brought him down to the floor gently without losing his purchase on the soft underside of the dog's jaw. Chemah spoke gently and moved his face close to that of the dog so that their eyes were six inches apart from each other. "Easy boy, no one is trying to hurt you. Easy. There, that's a good boy."

Chemah loosened the grip he had on the dog's lower jowls, but kept his face in front of the dog's and continued to talk gently to him. "You're a good boy," he said to the dog. "A good boy." Michelle did not know what had happened, but Keith, who had been hanging back about twenty feet or so, had seen the whole thing. He'd never seen a human being move as fast as he'd seen Chemah move. Chemah hadn't even flinched when the dog lunged at him and he seemed to have caught the dog without even having looked in his direction.

Keith had heard the legends of some of Chemah's exploits when he was in the police academy and had chalked up some of the stories to overzealous imaginations. What he'd seen was the stuff those stories were made of: unbelievable shit.

Michelle had heard the low growl before Base had leapt at Chemah and was concerned. "Are you all right, Detective Rivers?" she asked Chemah, having experienced the aftermath of that low growl before. Michelle was thrusting her hand out, patting at the air frantically in search of her best friend. Base came forward the two steps he needed to put his head under her hand.

When Michelle's hand found Base's head she was startled to find another hand already rubbing the spot on Base's scalp that he enjoyed having massaged. Michelle didn't pull her hand away. She allowed her hand to accidentally touch Chemah's while she feigned petting her dog. I was right, Michelle thought as the back of her hand touched Chemah's and felt the tautness of his skin. He *is* a young man. The urge to reach up and touch his face was almost overwhelming, but Michelle satisfied herself by openly touching his hand without pretense.

"You have very strong hands, Detective Rivers," she said, massaging the moisture of her hand into his own. Chemah didn't feel Michelle was doing anything wrong. After all, she was blind and this was the way that blind people made associations; through touch, hearing, and smell. He was, however, embarrassed for his own part in the situation. He was enjoying the way Michelle was touching his hand and felt he was somehow taking advantage of her. When Michelle had memorized every crevice of his hand, she lovingly placed it back on his chest. The subtle way that she did it allowed her to feel the muscle in his chest without conveying any flirtatiousness or impropriety. She was obviously both—flirty and improper—she thought to herself, feeling the moisture seep into her panties.

Chemah was fighting the hardness he felt creeping into his pants again and bent one knee to the floor again to pet the dog.

"What's his name?" Chemah asked Michelle as he briskly rubbed the dog's back.

"His name is Base," Michelle responded, not knowing if she had disgusted Chemah with her behavior or her appearance.

"He's a great dog," Chemah said, making idle conversation so that he wouldn't have to let this beautiful blind woman go.

"You must really have a way with animals," Michelle said, having the same motive as Chemah. "Base never lets anyone pet him. Even real dog lovers find it hard to appreciate him."

"This dog? Nah, I can't believe that," Chemah said, lying. He knew the dog was a killer and the dog knew it about him, too. Their mutual respect was all that was keeping one from hurting the other.

After a moment, Chemah got back on his feet. "Excuse me one second, Ms. Thomas, I have to arrange for your ride back home." Chemah walked over to the desk sergeant and spoke to him briefly while Michelle waited with Base by the bench. "It's all arranged, Ms. Thomas," Chemah said when he returned to Michelle's side. " Have a seat right here for a few minutes," he said, taking the opportunity to touch her hand again and guided her to the bench two feet behind her.

Base moved lazily to lay by Michelle's feet, but did nothing more. "The two officers that picked you up are going to be taking you back home," he said. "I hope we didn't take up too much of your time, Ms. Thomas," he added, stalling for more time with her.

"Michelle," the young blind woman said, desperate to continue feeling Chemah's presence.

"Pardon me?" Chemah asked.

"Michelle," she said again. "You keep calling me 'Ms. Thomas' and I expect to hear my mother's voice calling me in for dinner," she explained.

Chemah smiled, appreciating Michelle's sense of humor. "All right, Michelle," Chemah was glad to be less formal. "I'm sorry I have to leave you now, but my partner seems to need me for something," he said, acknowledging Keith, who was waving a stack of papers at him from the doorway of the homicide detectives' office. "I hope to see you again soon," Chemah said, walking away.

"Well, you know what the one-eyed prostitute said to her date?" Michelle said to Chemah's back.

"Pardon me," Chemah said, not having quite heard what Michelle had said.

"I'll keep an eye out for you," Michelle said, winking toward the sound of Chemah's voice.

Chapter 5
LADY SINGS THE BLUES

Margarita was in her cell contemplating the last three years of her life. She looked at herself in the shiny piece of metal that hung on her wall acting as a mirror. Her hair had finally grown back to its normal shoulder length. Her dark brown skin was radiant today, she thought. It was a testament to how she felt inside. Her body felt strong now after lifting weights daily for three years, as opposed to when she first came in and had the slim figure of a model.

Her jail family had been coming by all day in a steady stream of visitors: mostly the Latina women who had taken her in and protected her when they found out she was Panamanian, and the younger women of color she had protected thereafter. She had been denying her heritage for most of her life, but here in the penitentiary, speaking Spanish had saved her. She hadn't known what to expect, but after three years in the penile system, she'd become a pro at maneuvering around and through the bullshit.

She didn't like to think about it now that she knew she'd be getting out soon, but if she'd had to spend her life in here, she knew she could run the whole prison. As it now stood, she had wrested a considerable amount of power from one of the toughest bitches in the place. She considered the life of the woman named Lolly—the woman who had befriended her on her first day in the system and had turned her out on that very same night. The woman who now lay dying in the hospital from wounds that Margarita had inflicted.

‡‡‡

On her first day in the pen Margarita was nervous and apprehensive about what to expect. She'd been sitting in a corner of the day room, watching television among other inmates when a giant bull dyke named Charli had approached her and unceremoniously informed her that she'd be the one eating her cunt out that night and every other night after that. Margarita was well aware that this type of behavior occurred in female prisons as she had witnessed it in the year that she'd spent on Rikers Island while going through trial. During that time, when she'd been invited to participate in a lesbian act, she'd tell the person that she was not interested and they'd go away.

When Margarita told Charli that she wasn't interested, Charli eased up next to her and began to whisper nasty shit that she was going to do to her into her ear. Although Margarita was afraid of the woman, she knew she had to take a stand before it went any further. Margarita got up from her seat determined to face Charli down. Charli anticipated the move and got up right along with her. Charli was a full foot taller than Margarita and looked down at her menacingly. Before Margarita was able to say anything, Lolly had strolled up alongside her and addressed Charli.

Lolly was approximately Margarita's height, but had a more muscular build, as if she worked out with weights regularly. She wore her hair in two plaits, and if it weren't for the scar over her left eye she'd have had the face of a model. "Are we having a problem here?" Lolly said, putting an arm around Margarita's shoulder as if they had been buddies for years.

Charli looked shaken, and answered Lolly before actually having gained her composure. "No Lolly, we're not having any problem. Are we, sweetheart?" She directed her question at Margarita.

"No, no problem at all," Margarita answered, not wanting any further problems.

Lolly continued to stare up at Charli until Charli looked so uncomfortable that she looked away and changed her posture, shifting her weight from her left side to her right and then back again.

"If you don't have anything else to say, then move the fuck along, Lurch."
Lolly said to the bigger woman.

Charli had a hurt look in her eye and bit her lip the way women do when
they're trying to stop themselves from crying. The big woman that had up
until that moment been portraying herself as the most masculine thug had
now been reduced to the basest example of a weak, emotional, and sniveling
woman with a few words and a look from Lolly.

"Sorry about that," Lolly said, taking her arm from around Margarita's shoulder
as she took notice of her discomfort. "Don't worry about her. She won't bother
you again if she knows you and I are friends," Lolly said. Lolly introduced herself to Margarita and after lunch introduced her to the rest of the set she
belonged to. Or the way Margarita observed it, the set that belonged to Lolly.

Margarita followed Lolly around the rest of the day. When it was time for
Lolly to report to her work detail she told Margarita to come along. Margarita
was leery of going. She didn't want to get into any beef with the correction
officers over being in an unauthorized area. It took Lolly a minute to convince
her that it would be no problem and true to her word the COs said nothing
to either one of the women as Lolly greeted the CO in the laundry room with
a nod of her head. Margarita's political background had accustomed her to
being in the presence of persons that wielded power and she easily recognized
the deference of the people who dealt with Lolly.

After evening chow Margarita was tired and decided she would lock in.
Lolly tried to get her to hang out in the day room, but Margarita begged off
and went back to her cell to sleep.

The singular *click* of a lone cell door opening was tantamount to a bell being
rung in the middle of a library. It was unnatural in this place where all doors
opened and closed simultaneously. Margarita's eyes opened immediately, but
she did not make any noise or move for fear that she would give away some
advantage. She couldn't tell what time it was because there was no window
that she could peer out of to gauge the moonlight. Margarita heard feet shuf-
fling in her cell before she heard the voice.

"Margarita. Pssst, Margarita, are you awake?" Relief passed over Margarita as she recognized Lolly's voice. She smiled to herself at her own paranoia and flipped over in her bunk, glad to greet her new friend. Margarita's smile turned to shit as she turned around and looked into the faces of four women. Lolly's face was one of them, the big dyke Charli was another, and she did not recognize the final two. Lolly was holding an ice pick under Margarita's neck and her lips were curled into a twisted and sadistic smile. The other three women jeered at Margarita over Lolly's shoulder, looking like hyenas waiting their turn at the slaughter of a lamb.

"Make one sound, bitch, and I shove this through your mouth and into your brain. You understand me?" Margarita silently nodded her head yes, and the gesture made Lolly's smile broaden.

"Sit up," Lolly ordered Margarita. Margarita did her bidding and sat up slowly, afraid to be poked by the cold piece of steel against her skin. "Take her clothes off of her," Lolly ordered the women behind her, stepping slightly to the side, but always keeping the ice pick under Margarita's chin.

Margarita closed her eyes as the women pounced on her. They took her pajama pants off first, then her top, and finally her panties.

"Now, let's see those tits," Margarita heard Lolly's voice say as she felt a cold hand reach behind her back and unsnap the fastener of her bra.

"Mmmmm, damn, those are pretty," one of the unidentified women said as the bra fell away.

After a moment, Margarita felt a weight other than her own on the bed. Then came a sickeningly sweet whisper from Lolly. "Open your eyes, Margarita, I have something for you, baby." Margarita heard the other women snicker and then she opened her eyes. Margarita stared into Lolly's shaved vagina. It was a fat, drooling cunt. The lips were swollen and hanging open. In the dimly lit cell, Margarita could make out the tattoo right above Lolly's pierced clitoris. It read *POISON*. Margarita's eyes bugged at the sight and she shook her head from side to side in disbelief of her predicament.

Lolly was delighted at her response and whispered to her again. "You can't believe your good luck, can you, baby? First night on the tier and already you get a sample of the prettiest pussy in the pen. Oh, just one warning, baby,"

Lolly said menacingly. "If I feel anything more than the playful nibble of your teeth on my pussy…you get this in your ear." Margarita felt the cold steel play on her earlobe and knew that Lolly was not bluffing.

Margarita swallowed down the revulsion she felt, as Lolly leaned her hips into her half-open mouth. She felt Lolly's wet, fleshy labia brush her lips and before she could move away, Lolly grabbed the back of her head with one hand and pulled it forward into her splayed cunt. Margarita closed her mouth and held her breath while Lolly ground into her face. When Margarita felt her nose slide into Lolly's wildly contracting hole, she was forced to open her mouth to breathe. Lolly continued her wild humping of Margarita's face for a full five minutes. The juices from her cunt were all over Margarita's face, dripping from her chin. Lolly's breath was coming in short gasps in time with her hip thrusts: "Uh uh uh uh uh uh uh. Stick your tongue out, baby, stick it out." Remembering the feel of cold steel, Margarita did as she was told. "Uh-huh, uh-huh, here it is, baby, here's Lolly's juice. Aaaaaaaaaaaaaaaaahhh! Shiiiiiiiiiiiiiiit!!!" Lolly convulsed into Margarita's face. It seemed to take an eternity for Lolly to stop shaking. Margarita felt herself go limp as Lolly released her head from a vise-like grip. Margarita was glad that the ordeal was over.

"She's all yours, ladies," Margarita heard Lolly announce. At this declaration the two still unidentified women lunged at Margarita. Each woman was holding down one of Margarita's arms and shoulders. Charli was between Margarita's legs before Margarita could get them closed. Margarita looked down between her own legs, willing them to close, as Charli used her massive arms to pry them farther apart. When Charli seemed to be satisfied that they were apart enough, she settled back on her haunches. Margarita was not mildly shocked when she saw what was fastened onto Charli's waist. It was a thick leather belt with a piece of wood attached to it. Margarita looked hard and was sure it was the end of a broom stick. Charli laughed when Margarita realized her intention and struggled harder against the two women holding her down. When the wood entered her, Margarita didn't scream. She bit her bottom lip until she could taste her own blood. She swore then and there that these women would die by her hand.

‡‡‡

Three of the four women were dead now. Lolly was in the infirmary. They didn't know if she was going to make it. Margarita was loathe to leave until she was sure that she had kept her promise to herself. She had done everything she could to get herself an early release. She'd had her lawyer contact powerful people that still owed her favors and other people whose secrets she had kept when she herself was in power. The pressure they'd put on the parole board had been enough to get her out without having to go to the board a second time. She'd done her minimum three years. The warden had questioned everyone personally about the tragic accident that had befallen the three women that died in the fire six months ago. It went on record as simply that, an accident.

Lolly, on the other hand, was a different story. Margarita had wanted to see the fear in her eyes as she died. Wanted her to know that she was the one taking her life. Setting Lolly up had been a work of art. Without her three henchmen Lolly's power had been fragile, and Margarita's jail family had gotten stronger. In the end it had been easy to catch her alone and plunge a pen into her eye. No one had heard Lolly scream and Margarita had taken her time beating her senseless.

The guard escorting Margarita out of the facility came to her cell. "Are you ready to go, Smith?" Margarita looked around her cell. She had not packed anything. She wanted no memories of this place.

"I'm ready," Margarita said, stepping out of the cell. "And it's *Ms.* Smith," she said, tossing her hair back, almost striking him in the face. "And don't you forget it."

Chapter 6

THE WORLD IS A GHETTO

Victor rose from an unfit sleep, still tired from his activities of the night before. His mother was already at the store, probably taking inventory, he guessed. Victor walked barefoot to the bathroom with his morning erection pressed hard against his Fruit of the Looms. He reached the toilet and pulled down his underwear. His penis pointed toward the ceiling. "Damn," he said, taking a step away from the toilet and pressing his penis down, attempting to aim at the toilet bowl. His urine arced toward the toilet, but his aim was off and it hit the back of the seat. Victor adjusted himself, taking another step back, and hit his mark.

The doorbell rang, interrupting his concentration and he jerked hitting the side of the toilet again. "Damn," he said again, not looking forward to cleaning his own urine off the seat. The doorbell rang again and Victor hurriedly finished his business. "I'm coming," he answered, walking on tiptoes across the cold floor.

Victor looked through the peephole and was surprised to see two police officers staring back at him through the convex glass. Victor hesitated as long as anybody else in the neighborhood would have at the sight of cops at their door

"Yes?" Victor asked the one-word question that cops knew meant, "What do you want?"

"Good morning, sir. We're canvassing the neighborhood and we were wondering if we could ask you some questions?"

Victor waited the necessary amount of time again and answered, "One minute, let me put some clothes on." Victor took his time getting dressed. He took about five minutes. He could have dressed faster, but wasn't in the mood to talk to anyone and was hoping that the police would get tired and walk away.

When Victor came back to the door he peered through the peephole again to make sure that the police had not left. When he saw that they were still waiting, he unlocked the two locks and undid the security chain that kept him and his mother safe.

"What's this all about, Officers?" Victor asked.

"Just a routine investigation," the shorter of the two cops answered. Victor knew that "routine investigation" was code for "We lookin' for a nigga that looks like you."

"Sir, where were you at about three a.m. this morning?" the tall African-American cop asked. "I was right here in my bed." Victor lied.

"Is there anyone that can vouch for that, son?" the black officer spoke again.

"Yes, my mother can vouch for me," Victor spoke to the black officer again. He looked at the stripes on the black officer's shirt and realized that he was asking the questions because he was the senior cop. From that point on Victor directed all his answers to him.

"Is your mother home now, and do you think we can speak to her?" he asked.

"My mom isn't here right now. We own the grocery store two blocks down to the right. She should be there right now. She'll tell you anything you want to know."

The black officer looked at him suspiciously, but Victor stared right back at him without blinking. His mother had trained him well against would-be conspirators.

"You Reesey Brown's boy?" said he asked, still looking suspicious.

"Yes I am," Victor said coldly, not liking the familiar way this man had mentioned his mother's name.

A smile came to the black officer's face. "Your mother and I grew up in the same neighborhood," the officer said. "She was the pride of our block. Everybody was in love with your mother," the officer said, still smiling.

When he noticed the sour look on Victor's face, he took an apologetic tone. "No disrespect, son, just an old man remembering younger days. Your Ma was always a good girl, never let anyone disrespect her. Man or woman, if I remember right."

Victor's gaze never faltered and it was disconcerting to the older black cop. He cleared his throat and continued: "Anyway, we don't have any more questions right now, but if you see anything strange, give us a call," and the cop handed him a card.

"You never said exactly what you were looking for," Victor said.

"Black man, five foot nine to six foot one, low haircut, wearing loose-fitting clothes," the young white officer spoke up.

"That could be anybody in Harlem," Victor said incredulously. "Thanks for your time, son," the older officer said. "Come on, Frank, we've got another hundred doorbells to ring."

Victor closed the door and listened for the officers to go away. They didn't. They rang one doorbell after another on his floor, talking to whoever answered the door. When they left his floor, he opened his door a crack to listen to them on the floor beneath his. They gave everyone the same rhetoric.

Victor closed the door and went back into his apartment. He started to put his clothes on hurriedly so that he could get down to the store to talk to his mother. He was sure the police officers didn't have anything on him, but it would raise a lot of suspicion if they did decide to go to his mother's store and confirm his whereabouts last night. His mother and he had actually gotten into their first real argument when he'd come home early this morning.

‡‡‡

Reesey had awakened from an agitated sleep in her own bed, with an itch between her legs. She knew what she needed to put herself to bed properly and tiptoed into her son's room with the intention of slipping under his covers and waking him with an oral massage. To her chagrin he was not in his bed. He must have snuck out the apartment after I went to bed, she'd thought.

Reesey walked to the kitchen to make herself a cup of tea. She took her first sip of tea and settled in a chair at the kitchen table. When Victor skulked back into the apartment at 3:10 a.m., trying not to wake his mother, that's where he found her.

"Where have you been?" Reesey had asked Victor before he could ask her what she was doing up at this hour.

"Just out," he'd said defensively, not liking the tone she was using with him. He was, after all, a grown man now.

"Just out," Reesey had mimicked him. "You come into this house at some ungodly hour, and when I ask you where you've been, all you can say is 'just out'?"

Victor was vaguely aware of his own anger and decided that it would be best to hash this out at another time. "Momma, I don't want to talk about this right now. I'm tired and I want to get some sleep."

Reesey had become livid at Victor's laissez-faire attitude. "You want to get some sleep, what about me? You think I can sleep with you out in those streets? Probably running down some little tramp to do whatever it is that you do with them," she'd said, not wanting to admit that he was doing to other women the same thing he was doing to her.

Running down some tramp, Victor had thought of the irony of what his mother had said. "I'm going to sleep," Victor had said, attempting to walk past his mother and into his room.

Reesey was strong and grabbed him by the arm, whipping him around to face her, as she had done many times before when he was a little boy. "Don't you walk away from me, boy," she'd said, daring him to take another step.

Victor had shrugged her hand off his arm and stared down into her eyes. "I ain't no boy, Momma, I've made up my mind of that." After a pause he'd said, "And I ain't your man, either, I've made up my mind of that, too."

Victor hadn't waited for a response from his mother; he'd turned again and gone to his room. Reesey had been distraught, she'd gone to her room and slammed the door behind her. *It was all those little hussies,* Reesey had screamed in her mind. After all she'd done. After forsaking her soul, the precise thing she had been trying to prevent had happened despite all of the measures she had taken. She had lain on her bed weeping and Victor could hear her through the thin wall that separated their rooms. He had almost gone into the room to console her, but thought it best to leave things as they were. He'd be moving on soon. And it would be easier this way.

‡‡‡

Victor walked slowly to his mother's store, not wanting to raise the attention of any of the uniformed police officers not ordinarily visible in the day, who he now saw combing the neighborhood. When he reached the store his mother was behind the register, giving change to an old woman from the purchase of a quart of milk.

"Have a good day, Ms. Jenkins," his mother said to the lady as she walked out the store. His mother looked at him and smiled kindly. He smiled back and decided that everything was going to be all right. He decided to go downstairs and finish up the inventory himself. He hadn't taken two steps toward the back of the store when his mother said, "The police were just here."

Victor turned around and noticed that her smile had broadened a little as he tried to hide his surprise. "What did they want?" he asked her, already knowing all too well.

"They wanted to know if you were home all night," Reesey said, the smile fading from her face.

Victor's throat was suddenly dry and he could not find enough spit to swallow. His eyes asked the question his dry lips could not utter. What had his mother told them?

"I told them you were home all night after we left the store."

Victor did not realize he had been holding his breath and let out a deep exhale at his mother's statement. "Thanks, Momma," he said and turned to go to the back of the store.

"Victor," his mother called out to him.

"Yes, ma'am?" Victor turned to face his mother again.

"Make sure you don't plan to go out again tonight. I'm making a special dinner for you tonight."

Victor's heart sank. He knew what the dessert would be. She had him right where she wanted him again. *I'll play this cat-and-mouse game for a while longer,* he thought, now taking a different view of his mother. His heart was hardened to her now. He felt trapped on all sides.

Chapter 7
GOTCHA

Three blocks away Chemah and Keith were debriefing the officers who had been sent out earlier to canvass the neighborhood. The night before there had been another murder. An officer on patrol had witnessed a man standing over the body. The officer called out to the man and the suspect ran. The police officer was out of shape and was unable to keep up with the suspect. Three blocks into the chase, the officer decided to call in backup. Unfortunately, it was a busy night and backup hadn't come fast enough. The chase had taken them into the outskirts of Harlem, 113th and Morningside Avenue. The suspect had been lost running through Morningside Park and there was now a dragnet over a three-block radius. Chemah lived approximately a mile and a half away on Sugar Hill, but it was still too close for comfort. He'd grown up on 121st Street and Lenox and still knew a lot of people on that side of town. He didn't like to do cases in his old neighborhood. He thought it was bad karma.

So far they hadn't turned up any leads. The neighborhood was like that. They wouldn't give up one of their own. The officers were out doing what they called "beating the bushes." That meant they had no leads and were simply out making some noise, trying to scare someone out into the open. Every officer they'd debriefed so far had come across at least ten men that fit the description of their suspect. That meant over two hundred suspects so far. There was no way they'd get away with calling in two hundred black men to do interviews.

The community wouldn't stand for it, and the department would not pay the overtime.

The last two officers who were to be debriefed came over to talk to Chemah and Keith. "Got anything?" Chemah asked the two officers standing in front of him.

The younger of the two cops happened to be a young white man. He looked eager enough, Chemah thought. "We've interviewed about twenty guys that fit the description, sir. We got nothing."

His partner, an older black cop, chimed in, "I think we've got one to look at."

His partner looked up at him in amazement. "Who?" the white cop asked.

"The kid whose mother owned the store," the older cop answered.

"We followed that up," the white cop said now, taking on an argumentative tone with his partner. "The kid checked out. His mother said he was with her at home all night."

The older officer ignored his partner's objections and spoke directly to Chemah as one parent speaks to another when they're talking about their children and the child they're speaking of is still in the room.

Chemah listened intently, ignoring the objections of the younger cop. "We talked to the kid, he said he was home all night. I knew the mother when we were kids. Good lady. Her father owned the store we used to all go to. She runs the place now. The lady had all the right upbringing, but she met the wrong guy and she had a couple of kids before he split. So I go over to check the kid's story and pay my respects. She was there putting boxes away and cleaning up the store. She had to stop a couple of times while we were there to take care of a couple of customers, but I got a chance to talk to her and she corroborates the kid's story. The kid didn't look like no druggie. He was the studious type. Good English and everything, like he was raised right."

Chemah's face lit up. The young white cop had listened to his partner's story and followed closely. He'd been there for the whole story that was told and had not found anything strange in the telling.

"We got one," Chemah said to Keith, who had also been listening to the story.

"We got one what?" Keith said, having heard the story and not finding anything unusual. He looked as perplexed as the white rookie in uniform. Chemah turned to his partner and tried not to sound condescending. This was why he liked to work alone. He didn't like explaining himself every minute.

"The family owns a store they've been working for years," Chemah began. Keith nodded his head indicating that he followed so far. "The kid's no crackhead. In fact, he's bright." Chemah looked to the older uniformed cop for confirmation. "His mom raised him right. Probably with the same work ethic that she got from her father." Keith continued to nod, but really didn't follow the train of thought. Chemah continued. "Then if that's so, why is the kid not in the store helping his mother out at one of the busiest times of the day? Why is he still at home sleeping or resting or whatever the fuck he was doing at home at ten o'clock in the morning? I'll tell you why. Because like any good mother, she saw that her boy was tired from his late night and she let him sleep. And like any good mother she lied for him when questions were asked about his whereabouts." Keith and the white rookie cop stared at each other as if to confirm each other's stupidity. *Why hadn't I thought of that,* they'd both thought.

The older black uniformed officer smiled. He knew Chemah would get it. They didn't come any sharper. "Here's the kid's name," the black officer said, tearing out a sheet from his memo book. "Do you want us to go with you to pick the kid up?"

"Pick him up for what?" Chemah said. "He hasn't done anything. We don't have anybody who can identify him." Chemah looked at Keith, willing him to keep his mouth closed. "And if he's as bright as you say, he's going to want to lawyer up before we can talk to him. No, we're going to let him go for a while. We'll keep an eye on him from a distance until he does something that we can use against him."

The other three men listening all nodded their heads in understanding, but the rookie officer in uniform was the only one who looked perplexed.

"Is there a problem?" Chemah asked, looking the man squarely in the eye.

The young officer seemed to have a problem speaking.

"Say whatever you have to say," Chemah allowed him.

"Sir, we're not even going to take him in for questioning?"

Chemah looked from the rookie to the senior officer. The senior officer looked away and toward the sky as if embarrassed for his partner's question. Chemah looked back to the rookie and purposely took a deep breath to calm himself. He was already feeling the pressure of not solving this case fast enough.

"Officer, if we were to take this guy in and he lawyered up before we could get anything out of him, he would be let go without so much as a slap on the wrist. On top of that, he would know we were on to him, and probably wouldn't make another move without looking over his shoulder twice. Or he'd leave town. Our chances of catching him would be slim to none. Do you understand?"

The rookie nodded his head vigorously, now aware that he had been the only one not onboard.

"And one last thing," Chemah said to the three cops still standing in front of him. "Nobody else but us knows we have somebody we're looking at, and I want to keep it that way. I'll tell the captain what we've got going on and I'm sure he'll agree." He was talking to the trio, but he was looking at the rookie. The rookie nodded his head again knowing that the speech was said just for him. Chemah shook the two uniformed cops' hands and thanked them for their help. He then got into the passenger side of the unmarked police car that he and Keith were riding. Chemah was excited. He tried to hide it, but Keith could see it on his face.

"You really think we've got our man?" Keith asked.

"I've been wrong before, but right now this is all we've got. I'll tell you one thing, though," Chemah said to Keith. "If it's not him, we're going to have another body on our hands real soon."

They had been working a lot of late nights and Keith looked exhausted, Chemah thought. He knew he was wearing the same haggard look and hoped it would be over soon. He thought of his kids and all the time he was missing with them.

Chapter 8
FIGHT THEN FLIGHT

Since Michelle had met Chemah, all she could think about was how wonderful he smelled. She thought about the feel of his hands and the sureness of his voice. It had been eight days and he still hadn't called her. There had been another killing some days ago and the news had said that they still had no leads. Michelle had been expecting that call at any moment, but it had never come. Chemah said he'd call her when they had a suspect for her to identify. Here it was, already Saturday, and she still had gotten no call. Chemah had been true to his word. No suspect. No reason to call.

Instead, she got a call from Karsem at six in the morning. He knew she was already up. And she gave in, telling him to be at her door in thirty minutes. She hadn't touched a man or herself since the day she had heard that woman being killed.

Michelle thought she'd made an impression on Chemah. She tried to be funny and smart and sexy all at once. Apparently it hadn't worked. Maybe it was the fact that she hadn't looked good or smelled good on the day that she had met him. She hadn't been showering for a couple of days and she hadn't made herself up. Who'd have known she would be meeting someone she might like? She tried not to pity herself. She was trying to convince herself it wasn't the blindness that turned him off. She wasn't trying to find a husband, after all, she only wanted to meet good, kind, and interesting people again.

She knew it was her fault that her friends and family didn't want to be around her. She'd pushed a lot of people away since she'd lost her sight. Michelle kept some of her old relationships, but none of the ones that had any significance. She'd felt goodness in Chemah. It was something she hadn't felt in herself in a long time, and now that she'd met Chemah, she wanted some of that goodness back. Michelle had slept well for the first time in days that first night after she'd met Chemah. She dreamed that she and Chemah would be a couple. That she would be with no other man but him and that he would find use for her in his life. It had been a stupid dream and she chastised herself. The dream of a little girl that accepted the physical love of strangers and said it was enough for her. Both her real life and her dreams were lies.

The doorbell rang and like always she knew it was Karsem. He was leaning into the doorbell as usual. Michelle started walking toward the door and then remembered that Base was still loose. She knew Karsem wouldn't come into her apartment until the dog was put into the bathroom and saw no use in prolonging the inevitable. After putting Base into the bathroom, she walked to the door, all the while trying to repress her dreams of Chemah.

She didn't know what Chemah looked like and didn't care at this point. Even if Chemah was a one-eyed gargoyle she still wanted to be near him. She had to find a way of talking to him again. She didn't know if he were married or if he had a girlfriend. When they met again, she would find all these things out. By the time she reached the door, she had resolved in her mind that this chapter in her life was over. She would not be experiencing "freelove" with Karsem this morning. *Even if I never meet with Chemah again, this is no way to live a life*, she thought.

Her experience that last day in the park had changed her forever, she decided. Life was too fragile a thing to go through so haphazardly. Karsem usually rang the bell more than once. Michelle almost hoped he wasn't at the door when she got to it. Normally, he would have rung again. He was always impatient to come in. Michelle began to open the door, but before she could get it fully open, it was pushed open the rest of the way.

Michelle stumbled backward and before she could right herself, she felt the full weight of a body crash against her, knocking her to the floor. It was Karsem's body, she knew immediately, as she pushed off against his head. She was familiar with the unique shape of his cranium, and was aghast and revolted as she felt how someone had changed its shape so dramatically at its base. Her hands were saturated with the sticky fluid that was gushing out of him and she tried to push herself away from the body and simultaneously wipe her hands off on the blouse she was wearing.

Michelle heard the door to her apartment close and then heard the lock turn as she got up from under Karsem's body. Before she could turn to run, she felt a foot hit her upper torso; it felt as though her chest had caved in as she hurled backward out of control. She came to a sudden stop as her body slammed into and then crumbled against the far wall. Michelle heard barking in the distance and briefly wondered why Base sounded so far away. She knew she was about to die. Strangely, she wasn't scared. The last thing she thought before she lost consciousness was, *Who's going to take care of my dog? After all, to the world you may be one person, but to one person you may be the world.*

‡‡‡

Michelle came to groggily aware that her attempts at movement were being inhibited. *I must be dead,* she thought to herself. She was listening to someone praying over her body. She was startled to full consciousness when she realized that she had heard that voice before. It was the voice from the park. She started to scream, but thought she would have to be more strategic than that, as she remembered the muffled scream of the woman with tape over her mouth that day in the park. She didn't feel anything around her legs yet. He was still binding her upper body.

Michelle tried to sense the proximity of the man who was standing over her. She would only have one chance and she had to make it count. When she thought the voice was right over her face she swung her leg up with all her might to where she thought his groin would be. Her leg sailed through the air and hit nothing. She had swung her leg so hard that she felt her own groin muscle pulled to its limit and she winced loudly with the pain, sure that she had torn something. She heard the prayer stop for a second and wondered how she could have missed.

A chuckle and an animal-like sound were emitted from the entity she had tried to kick. Michelle realized in despair that she had not simply miscalculated, she had depended too much on her hearing. The killer's face had indeed been in front of hers, the problem had been that the rest of his body had been above her head. The cost of her mistake was her life and the thought of that made her angry.

"You think that was funny, do you?" she said to the voice that had started his prayers again. "I've got another funny one for you," she said to the whispering prayer. The praying stopped momentarily. "Knock, knock," Michelle said out loud. There was no answer. Michelle got louder. "Knock, knock, motherfucker," she said louder this time.

The voice hesitated, then responded softly, "Who's there?" Despite her plight, Michelle was forced to smile a little. "Tijuana," she said evenly.

"Tijuana who?" the voice continued to play along.

"Tijuana, take your mother to the gang-bang?" Michelle laughed loudly at her own joke. She was in good humor for about three seconds until she felt a fist smash into her right cheek.

Michelle yelped and tried in vain to sit up. She heard a grunt of approval from her captor and settled back down, her mind reeling from trying to find a way out of this.

"What's the matter, you didn't like that one?" Michelle played a hunch. "It was the momma thing, wasn't it? I'm sorry, I didn't mean to say anything bad about your mother."

Michelle was stalling for time, trying to remember all of the snaps and ranking she and her friends had antagonized one another with. The worst thing that could come out of your mouth on her block always started with "yo mama." Some neighborhoods had rules against talking about each other's mothers when trading insults. Her neighborhood had no such rule—they went straight for the jugular—and she had been the worst of them all.

"Listen, you can let me go. I don't know what you look like, I can't ID you, or your mother. All I ever heard about her is that she's like a postage stamp: lick her, stick her, and then send her away."

Michelle heard a grunt from her assailant, not the response that she wanted.

"No, that wasn't it. That's not what I heard. I heard she was walking down the street with a mattress strapped to her back asking for volunteers." Michelle was used to acting when she was doing her stand-up routine and she forced herself to giggle and teehee at her own jokes.

"Whoa, ho ho ho ho, that was a good one," she said, acting as if she were amusing herself to pass the time. "Yeah, that bitch is like peanut butter, she spreads easy."

The taping of the rest of her arms had ceased and that was what she wanted. "I ain't one to talk, but I heard your mother was stupid. She was so stupid she got fired from a blow job." She forced herself to laugh at her own joke again, as silly as it was. "Yo mama is so stupid, I heard she went to the movies 'cause she heard they were selling Free Willies...." Michelle waited for a response and got a punch in the face in return. She laughed at the punch almost deliriously.

"Was that a punch, bitch?" she said, spitting out blood with her words. "Shit, your mother's twice the man you are. Like I was getting ready to say, before I was so rudely interrupted." She paused for a moment to spit more blood. "I was walking down the street with your mother and they started shooting. Somebody said 'hit the dirt,' and everyone jumped on your mother's back."

After her last words, Michelle had expected another hit. She even flinched when she felt the killer move above her. She felt him walk away and breathed a sigh of relief. She was getting a moment's reprieve.

If she had known where he was going she would not have breathed so easily. Her assailant was walking down the hall to where he had dropped the hammer that he had struck Karsem with. He was tired of all her talking and was going to beat her teeth down her throat. Praying for her might even have to wait until he shut her up for good. She didn't seem like the repentant type and allowing her to beg the Lord's forgiveness would be a waste of time, he thought as he picked up the hammer. The weight of the hammer in his hand made him feel good again and he started walking back to the whore.

‡‡‡

Michelle was breathing hard. The last punch she took had shaken her more than she had let on. At least she wasn't being tied up anymore, she thought. She didn't know what she was waiting for. She knew there would be no knight in shining armor to save her. She had to act now. Michelle scrambled to her feet and staggered back and forth as if moving on the deck of a ship. In her disoriented condition Michelle took two steps and smashed her face into the wall to the left of the living room door. As she shook off the effects of the jarring hit, she heard the same sinister chuckle she'd heard earlier when she'd tried to kick her assailant. Michelle took two tentative steps backward and the back of her leg touched her living room couch. *At least I know where I am now,* she thought.

Michelle had no way of defending herself with her arms taped to her sides. The best defense is a good offense, she remembered her father saying. She decided she would wait till he was close enough, then she would put her head down and ram him. Michelle's keen hearing detected him taking a second step into the room and she put her head down to charge. Before she could get a running start, she heard a loud grunting "aaaaarrghh" and then furniture started to move. It was Karsem. She deciphered his voice through the grunts and curses. It only took moments before Michelle heard the hammer landing. It was like the sound a potted plant might make when it crashes to the floor. Except this sound came to Michelle's ears a dozen times in a row.

Michelle crashed her shoulder into the wall to the right of the doorway in a rush to get away from the wet sucking sound the hammer made each time it was extracted from Karsem's head. She slid her body against the wall looking for the opening and stumbled out into open space a second later. She knew exactly where she was now, but she could hear the killer's steps a moment behind her. She knew she had only one chance. She turned the corner of the hallway and ran as fast as she could with her head down. The killer stopped chasing, thinking that she had run the wrong way, opposite the apartment door. *Stupid whore,* he thought, as he watched her pick up speed. He was amused at the stupidity of these women. *They deserve to die,* he thought. When Michelle's body hit the bathroom door, it nearly exploded off the hinges.

Michelle lay unconscious on the cool marble of the bathroom floor and didn't see what happened next. Base was loose. He stood over Michelle's motionless body for a moment before sensing someone else moving in the apartment. Base darted out of the bathroom door and saw the killer at the same time that the killer saw him. Base gave one low growl as a warning (his calling card before attacking). Base came bounding down the hall looking as fiendish as a hound from hell. The killer raised his hammer, readying himself for Base's attack, but at the last moment his cowardice gave him away. The sight of him standing there with his hammer raised struck no fear into the charging dog; the beast was, after all, no helpless female. The killer second-guessed himself and turned to look for an escape route. That was his undoing.

In that split second, he knew running was no longer an option, but the pause had given Base time to take flight. Base was in the air with his jaws open wide when the killer turned to face him again. As Base reached him the killer's fear made him swing the hammer too soon. Base was hit with a glancing blow to the snout. As Base hit the floor, the killer swung the hammer at him again, but Base had been too quick and the blow never landed. Base jumped up at the killer's swinging arm and bit down hard on his forearm. If the killer had not been wearing a leather jacket Base might have drawn blood. As it was the pressure that Base's jaws were applying forced the killer to drop his hammer. The killer tried to beat Base off with his free hand, but Base continued to hold on. The killer almost attempted to kick Base away from him, but he thought better of it. What if he did kick the dog off him? The dog would still continue to attack and next time he might get a hold of his neck.

The killer finally started to drag himself and Base toward the apartment door. The killer pulled hard again and felt Base's grip slip. Now Base only had a piece of jacket in his teeth. The killer counted to himself, one, two, three. He raised his right knee up to his own chest and then pushed out with his foot as hard and fast as he could. Base's grip on the leather did not falter, but the jacket tore and Base was knocked back through the air. Base landed on his back, but jumped up on all fours again and without hesitation ran at his master's assailant again. Base was half a second too late. When the killer kicked Base away he'd already had one hand on the doorknob. Before Base had hit the floor he'd already flung the door open and bolted. He had turned and slammed the door at the very moment Base went airborne again. He heard the dog crash against the door and thought maybe the dog had knocked himself out. The killer leaned against the door and listened carefully. He heard deep breathing. The dog wasn't knocked out, he was merely waiting.

The killer heard a door open on the floor above where he stood and knew it was time to leave. It wouldn't do to have anyone see him here. He left, cursing at the dog under his breath. Base was on the other side of the door waiting. The next person to enter the apartment was sure to get bitten.

Chapter 9
PULL YOUR SKIRT DOWN

Chemah wasn't told of the attack on Michelle until he walked into his office on Monday morning.

"Where is she?" Chemah nearly shouted at Keith, who was keeping his own voice low in an attempt to keep Chemah calm and reasonable, like him. It had the opposite effect. "Where is she?" Chemah's voice was now low, too, but there was no calmness in it, and his face held no sign of reasoning. Chemah didn't lose his temper often, but when he did there was no reasoning with him. "Who the fuck made the decision not to call me the minute this happened?"

Keith swallowed hard and answered up. "They called me about it Saturday afternoon. They said they couldn't get you. You weren't answering your cell, so I made an administrative decision. I knew we had Kelly and Jones outside of the Brown kid's apartment and they hadn't called in to report anything special, so I figured it was an unrelated attack. There was no indication that the 'Street Sweeper' had anything to do with this."

"The 'Street Sweeper'?" Chemah asked, his voice was almost inaudible. "Who the hell is the 'Street Sweeper'?"

"That's the name the media has given the killer," Keith explained. "I think it fits," Keith said matter-of-factly. "The media says fewer women have been staying out late since…" Keith didn't finish his sentence. He saw the look on Chemah's face and swallowed his words.

Chemah looked around the office, aware that he could not tell his new partner what he really thought in the presence of the other detectives there. The eyes of all the detectives in the room were on him. Chemah knew that none of the other detectives liked Keith. He was the only one who had not earned his place here and for that reason he was resented. Chemah knew his role as a leader among his peers and knew they'd follow his lead depending on how he treated Keith. He hated dissension in the ranks and didn't want to give anyone more ammunition against Keith than they already had.

"Come with me," Chemah said to Keith, leading the way out of the office.

Keith pursed his lips in defiance, but followed Chemah anyway. "This is some bullshit," he said under his breath.

Chemah led Keith to one of the interview rooms. He opened the door, held it open for Keith, and then locked it behind them when Keith stepped over the threshold.

"Listen, man," Keith began, "if you think you're going to kick my ass, you can forget it. I've got a black belt in karate, tae kwan do, and juijitsu, and the last nigga who stepped to me is still recuperating."

Chemah stared at Keith in disbelief.

"Well, what you got?" Keith said, taking a fighting posture.

Chemah walked to the table on the opposite side of the room and sat on its edge. "Do you think this is some sort of game?" he said to Keith in a low, dangerous tone. "There are people dying out there." Chemah paused for a second. "I brought you in here so that we could talk this out like two grown men with differences. We're partners now, like it or not, and we have to work together. If anyone out there sees us having problems, we're fucked. Divide and conquer, or haven't you heard, there are only five black detectives in this unit. Not counting the captain. We have to be twice as good as the other guy in order to get the same respect." Chemah paused again to see if his point had reached his partner.

"I'm not going to sugarcoat it, man, you fucked up this weekend. You are in no position to make administrative decisions. We may be partners, but make no mistake about it, I call all the shots on this case. And if I'm not around, you'd better make damn sure you find the captain and ask him what you should do, because he doesn't like you any more than the perps out there do. He's looking for a reason to put your ass back in uniform and send you back to writing tickets."

Keith looked thoroughly ashamed.

"I'm going to take the hit for this one," Chemah said a little more softly now. "The captain is going to know that it wasn't me that made the decision to come in on the weekend call, but I'll insist that it was my bad. It'll take the weight off you for a minute, and believe me when I say a minute, I mean it. The captain's no fool. After this fuckup, he's gonna be on your ass like it was the last helicopter out of Vietnam."

Chemah walked over to Keith and patted him on the back. "Keep your head up, son, it's only going to get worse." The two men exchanged smiles and then shook hands in what looked like the secret handshake from some fraternal order, both ending with their right hands over their hearts. Chemah turned to leave but Keith stopped him.

"I have to know," Keith said.

"You have to know what?" Chemah asked, knowing precisely what the kid was asking.

"Is your knuckle game as tight as they say it is?" Keith asked.

Chemah smiled a devious smile and said, "The stories are always better than the real thing."

Chemah started to turn toward the door again and saw the blur of movement that was Keith's fist. In his mind he could have blocked it, but at the speed the fist was moving it would have incapacitated Keith's arm for a while. Everyone would know the kid had been reckless, and that would not do. Instead, Chemah allowed the fist to go by him. That was the first one, then another, and another, and another. Chemah deceptively moved his hands using the style he had developed some years before called the Fifty-two Steps of *Goju*. Chemah's hands never touched Keith, but their movement blinded him momentarily and he stopped throwing punches.

Keith took a quick step back and smiled at Chemah. "That was pretty good," he said, proud that he had caused Chemah to be on the defensive. "Of course, it's one thing to be able to get out of the way of punches and another thing to be able to hit someone," Keith said, getting in a defensive posture. He was ready to prove he could hang with the best.

Chemah looked at Keith quizzically and raised his right fist up very slowly to chest level. Keith bore down even harder, now sure that he was ready for anything. Chemah smiled at this young man's spirit and turned his fist over, palm upward.

Chemah opened his hand to display five buttons. Keith looked at the buttons and for a second did not comprehend. Chemah motioned down to Keith's chest and Keith looked down and stared at his exposed midriff. He looked back up at Chemah and caught the twinkle in his eye.

"When you can, snatch these buttons from my hands, then you'll be ready to leave the monastery, Grasshopper," Chemah said, imitating a scene from David Carradine's *Kung Fu* TV series. Chemah laughed at his own little joke and opened the door to leave.

Keith pulled the two parts of his shirt together, trying to hide the evidence of his mistake. "Hey man, give me my buttons back," he called after Chemah, who was halfway down the hall already.

Chemah only laughed and kept walking. "I'm not joking, man, give me back my buttons, this was an expensive shirt."

Keith chased after Chemah, who continued to walk down the hall, but he stopped laughing. He was thinking about Michelle again. He had to get to the hospital.

Chapter 10
KILLING HER SOFTLY

C hemah went to the hospital alone. He had been right. The captain had not believed his and Keith's story. When he had left, the captain had still been ripping Keith a new asshole. Chemah knew the captain would be giving Keith all of the menial tasks that you could give a detective and still be within the guidelines of the job description. Chemah had tried his best to protect him, but it hadn't worked out. Chemah had given Keith dap and told him that he would catch him later on that day. Keith had looked like a puppy whose balls had been taken.

Chemah had found out the floor and room number that Michelle was in before he'd left the precinct, but when he got off the elevator he was unsure of which way to go. There were two rooms parallel to each other that had uniformed officers posted at the doorway. Chemah went toward the door closest to him and the officers at the door got up from their seats as soon as they saw the gold shield on his lapel. The officers at the door saluted him and he saluted back. Chemah recognized them as rookies, as only new officers ever saluted detectives.

"Is Michelle Thomas in this room?" Chemah asked the officer who stood directly in front of the door.

"Yes, sir," the young officer said, stepping to the side.

Chemah knocked on the door twice and then went in. Michelle was sitting up in her bed, smiling at the wall directly in front of her when Chemah entered the room. She didn't turn her head at the sound of the door opening and Chemah wondered what she was smiling about. As Chemah reached the side of her bed, Michelle turned her head to the exact spot where he was standing and addressed him with a big smile. "Hello, Chemah," she said, still maintaining her smile.

Chemah winced when he saw the left side of her face. She had a welt on her cheekbone the size and color of a plum. He tried to hide the emotion he felt well up in his throat at the sight of Michelle's injury and swallowed hard. He tried to greet her as cheerfully as he could muster. "Hello, Michelle," was all he could get out, his anger catching like wildfire.

"Hmmm, that doesn't sound like the Detective Rivers I met the other day," Michelle said. "The Detective Rivers I met was surer of himself, more energetic, more vibrant. Now let's try this again," Michelle said. "From the top. I'll go first. Hey, Chemah, what's crackin'?"

Chemah played along. "It's all good, baby, all good. You lookin' fine as ever. I see you sportin' that new color blush."

At those words, Michelle touched her cheek where the purple was deepest. It was a stupid joke and Chemah regretted saying it. Michelle continued to smile, but Chemah was not fooled. Chemah took her hand away from where she was touching the welt and replaced it with his own. He stroked the purple bruise softly and Michelle closed her eyes, enjoying the feeling of his tender caress. The bruise was so deep that it hurt no matter how delicately Chemah touched it, but Michelle would not have told him to stop no matter how much it hurt. There was an intense pleasure in her pain and she wallowed in it.

Chemah didn't know what possessed him to touch this woman like this. He barely knew her and it was the worst professional mistake a detective could make, getting involved with a witness. He had felt an immediate attraction to her the first time he met her, but had dismissed it as a severe case of desert dick. After all, it had been three years since his penis had seen any moisture. This woman was like an oasis after those long, hard, and lonely years. Chemah stopped caressing Michelle's face and her eyelids immediately popped opened. Her mouth was about to form words, but Chemah finished her thought for her. "Don't worry, I'm not going anywhere," he informed her. Michelle relaxed her head back into the pillow, a lazy smile playing across her face.

Chemah pulled a chair up next to her bed and held her hand. They talked to each other for one hour after the other. First they talked about Michelle's father and her entire family, and then they talked about Chemah's two children and the problems he had encountered in raising them. When Chemah talked about them, he glowed. Michelle couldn't see it, but she could feel the passion and joy that came from his voice when he described their antics.

The conversation was never lopsided. One always deferred to the other, only stopping when a doctor or nurse came in to check on Michelle's injuries. At some point in their conversation, Chemah noticed that he was not holding her hand as much as she was holding his. It felt good having a woman touch him again. Michelle had reached back into his memory and touched a part of him he'd thought was long dead. It was a part that only one other woman had touched. It was his soul. It was only after the death of his son's mother that Chemah came to believe in soul mates. And when his son's mother had died he believed that he would never find another woman to take her place. He had been married to his ex-wife Margarita at the time and every moment he had spent with her after that seemed to make his soul grow colder and colder. His children and his job were the only two things that kept him going.

‡‡‡

During their day at the hospital together, Chemah had learned that Michelle would be released the next day. A thought occurred to him. She needed to be in a witness protection program. A safe house. Where would there be a house safer than his? The day at the hospital was nearly spent and Chemah had not once broached the subject of Michelle's attacker. It was now seven o'clock at night; he had his children at home with a sitter and he would have to leave shortly.

"Michelle, I've been thinking, how would you like to come home with me tomorrow?" Chemah finally began.

Michelle's smile was instant and then her brow creased and furrowed. "You think he'll come after me again, don't you?" Michelle asked.

Chemah nodded yes, forgetting for a moment that she couldn't see.

"Is that it? Is that why?" she asked again. Chemah answered with a sad "yes," and was doubly sad when tears came to Michelle's eyes.

For a man who was so quick-witted and astute, Chemah was clueless when it came to reading women. It was an unforgivable sin. He did not recognize that Michelle was not upset because she thought that the killer was still after her. She was upset because the only reason that he had asked her to come stay with him after all the time and feelings they had shared on that day was because it was his job. The reason Chemah had actually asked her was much more than that, but he didn't know that she needed to hear those other reasons. Otherwise he would surely have voiced his longing to have her by his side.

It took Chemah another half hour to convince her that the best thing to do would be to stay with him. She was scared of going back to her apartment, but her pride would not allow her to stay with this man that she was falling in love with because he felt sorry for her and it was his job to protect her. Ultimately he convinced her that she should do it for Base, who she had explained to him earlier was still being held in the custody of the ASPCA. One of her neighbors had heard the commotion in her apartment and came down only to find the door unlocked. Not suspecting that there was a ferocious dog waiting for him on the other side, he had opened it and almost lost an arm. Michelle had a visit from another neighbor yesterday, and she'd been informed that some of her other neighbors were passing around a petition to keep her dog out of the building. Michelle thought she could fight her neighbors in court, but it might be best to keep Base out of sight for a while.

"What about your children?" Michelle asked. "Won't they be disturbed, to find a blind woman intruding on their lives?"

Chemah seemed to be thinking for a moment and then said, "No. Anyway, I don't think so," he contradicted himself.

Michelle finally saw the flaw in this man who she was coming to think was perfect. His observational skills were beyond normal, he could detect things that the average person would find impossible to uncover, but when it came to people who he cared about, he was dense. There was something in him that allowed him to be insensitive to the people that were closest to him. He either didn't want to feel their pain, or didn't want to get used to their love, she guessed. She didn't think that she presumed too much, believing that he did feel something for her already. He had shown a good deal of concern and tenderness for her today, from the moment he entered her room. And she had thought there was something between them the first day that they'd met. The time she had flirted with him, unashamedly touching his hand and chest...

Michelle agreed to leave with him the next morning. Like all women, she thought she could change him in time. The feelings were there, after all. All he needed was some training. Chemah agreed to pick her dog up from the ASPCA before coming to get her. Michelle didn't want her best friend to stay locked up any longer than was necessary and Chemah was the only one who could get away with handling him, besides her. It was all set. All he had to do was convince the captain.

Chapter 11
White Chocolate

hemah walked out of Michelle's hospital room and caught sight of his captain entering the room parallel to Michelle's. He was about to call out to him, but instead walked the few extra steps to the door and asked the officers standing on either side of the door who it was they were guarding. These were not the same officers who had been standing guard when he entered Michelle's room earlier that day. They weren't rookies. They recognized Chemah and greeted him as a comrade, shaking his hand and talking freely.

"It's some guy named Robert O'Malley, they say he works forensics," the taller of the two officers said.

"Black Rob?" Chemah asked, hoping he wasn't right.

"Yeah, that's him," the shorter officer said. "There was another guy who came in earlier and called him that."

Chemah didn't wait for any more information. Rob was a good friend of his. He wasn't a cop, but he was the best lab tech Chemah ever knew. Rob had done Chemah many favors, and he was the only tech who allowed Chemah to work alongside him. Earlier in their relationship, Chemah had even trained him in martial arts. He was one of those good guys that you could always count on. Rob had only one significant character defect that Chemah could see. He wanted to be black. He dressed in clothes that were stereotypically black, he faded his hair like a black man, and he spoke in ebonics all the time. Chemah had found out that he'd even dated black women all his life. The only reason he had eventually dated and finally married a white woman was that he saw that a lot of other black men wanted to get with white women, and he wanted to know what it was like. He even found one with a big fat ass.

Chemah walked into the room tentatively scared of what he'd find. Both the captain and Rob turned toward the door at the same time. Rob smiled happily. The captain didn't. Chemah could see instantly that Rob was going to be okay.

"Aaaaah, shit. That's my knucka right there, 'nam sayin', my nigga if I don't get no bigga."

Chemah winced, knowing the captain would not appreciate Rob's use of the word "nigga."

The captain looked at Chemah as if waiting for him to respond to a white man's use of that term. Chemah acted as if he had not heard anything out of place and gave his boy a pound. Of course, Rob turned the handshake into a spectacle that would make a gang member envious, but Chemah ignored this, too. He'd had many talks with Rob about the professional inappropriateness of anyone using the word "nigga," or "nigger," but nothing had changed.

Chemah turned his attention to the captain. "Hey, Cap, anything new?" he said.

"We'll talk outside in a minute," the captain said.

Chemah nodded, knowing it wouldn't be a pleasant conversation. "So, one of your girlfriends finally tried to kill you?" Chemah asked, trying to open a line of conversation that would allow him to find out what had happened to his friend.

"Yo, son, I can't be faded, you know what Pac said." Rob grinned up at him. "No matter how you try, niggas never die. We retaliate with hate and then we multiply."

The captain looked like he was about to pull his hair out. Chemah pressed on with his questions, knowing that the captain was not here for a friendly visit.

"What really happened, Rob?" Chemah asked. The seriousness in Chemah's voice made Rob stop smiling. He looked at the captain, then back to Chemah.

"It's like I told those clowns earlier today, son. I was checking the DNA of four different blood types that were found in that rape assault that happened over the weekend."

Chemah glanced quickly at the captain for confirmation.

"That's just what they were calling it," the captain said, allaying Chemah's fears. "They didn't know what we know, and that's because everyone thinks they're running their own fucking precinct, no one has the right information."

Rob rubbed his head. "Yeah, whatever. All I know is I was looking under a microscope one minute and then I woke up here."

"You mean you never saw who hit you ?" Chemah asked.

"Yo, son, you know I'm about handling my bidness, if a nigga woulda stepped to me man to man, you'da been comin' ta see someone else in the hospital, na'mean?"

The captain looked furious. "What the fuck did he say?" He looked like he was about to attack Rob himself. Rob saw the danger in the captain's eyes and pulled the hospital sheets up under his chin as if that would protect him.

Chemah put his hand up, signaling the captain to calm down so that he could continue to question Rob. "Rob, was there anyone else around you or were you talking to any one else before you were knocked out?" Chemah asked.

Rob shook his head no, and answered, "Nah, a brotha was solo the whole time, ya dig?" he said, never once taking his eyes off the captain.

"One last thing, Rob," Chemah said, reaching out to pull Rob's face toward him and away from the glowering captain. "Is there anything you can tell us about the blood that was found on the scene?"

Rob blinked twice as if to see Chemah more clearly now.

"Yeah, there's something. I identified three of the samples. One belonged to the victim, one belonged to the dead guy in the apartment, and another belonged to the guy that found the victim."

"You mean the upstairs neighbor?" Chemah said.

"I guess," Rob said and shrugged. "The fourth blood sample might be the attacker. It didn't belong to anybody that was there when you boys showed up," Rob surmised.

"Then all we have to do is find out who the blood sample belongs to." Chemah sighed with relief.

The captain was shaking his head. "That's going to be impossible," he said.

"That's the reason I'm here. The evidence that was taken from that site, including the blood sample, is gone. Whoever beat Rob here in the head also took the samples. Internal Affairs is on their way over here. They have questions for him," the captain said, pointing to Rob.

"Me, what do they want with me?" Rob said, sounding as Caucasian as Chemah had ever heard him.

"They want to know what happened to that evidence and you're the last person that saw it," the captain said.

"But I'm the one with the bump on my head," Rob said, looking scared.

"This shit is bigger than any of us," the captain said. "When I figured out what actually happened over the weekend I had to report to my superiors, too. Everybody has to be accountable. Now this evidence is missing on my watch and my dick is swinging in the wind. So if there's anything you forgot to tell us, you damn well better remember it before IAD gets here," the captain finished, reaching over the bed and jabbing Rob in the chest.

Rob went farther under the hospital sheets, trying to get away from the captain's finger.

"Anything, Rob?" Chemah asked, but Rob shook his head no dejectedly.

"Captain, can I talk to you outside?" Chemah asked. The captain walked out of the room and Chemah followed without exchanging any more words.

The captain and Chemah took the elevator all the way down to the lobby before either of them said anything again.

"Captain, you know Rob had nothing to do with what happened," Chemah said.

The captain pulled out a cigar and put it in his mouth as he started to walk out the building. "Yeah, I know," the captain said, smiling through the cigar in his mouth.

Chemah caught on quickly. "IAD isn't coming down, are they?"

"Nope." The captain's smile broadened even farther.

"Then you were simply fucking with Rob the entire time?"

"Yep," the captain answered.

Chemah blew out a deep breath and wiped non-existent sweat from his brow.

The captain turned to Chemah as they reached the curb. "I would have given you and your partner the assignment of interviewing Rob, if I hadn't already given Medlin fifty or so bullshit assignments to keep him out of your hair for a while. Something wrong with your cellphone, you not answering it?" the captain asked.

"Must be. You're the second person who's asked me that. It could be this bullshit service I have that keeps dropping phone calls," Chemah answered.

"Whatever it is, get it fixed. I have to be able to contact you at all times. You see the shit that happened this weekend without us being around?"

Chemah nodded his head yes. "I'll take care of it, boss."

"Good." The captain seemed tickled. "So, how do you think your boy liked a real dose of being black?"

Chemah laughed. "You know that's not going to change him, right, Captain?

"Yeah, I know, but it sure as hell made me feel good," the captain said, chuckling to himself again. The captain was having such a good time with his little joke that Chemah didn't want to change his good mood by telling him about his witness protection plan with Michelle. He knew the captain would agree to anything he thought was right, but he would still have to sell him on the idea. He and the captain had a history together and they both knew you couldn't always go by the book. This would have to be one of those times.

Chapter 12
MI CASA, SU CASA

hemah was in the small backyard of the brownstone trying to convince Base to be quiet. Base wasn't used to being outdoors on his own. As soon as he smelled the scent of another dog in one of the backyards a few houses away, he started barking so loudly, Chemah thought his neighbors might start complaining. He was trying to calm Base down, but Base would only remain quiet while Chemah was there with him. Every time Chemah tried to leave, Base would start to bark again.

Michelle was sitting on Chemah's living room couch. She had finished unpacking the few items that she had asked Chemah to pick up from her apartment, and then made her way back downstairs. She took a few minutes trying to memorize where some of the furnishings were and then plopped down on the couch to wait for Chemah to make her some lunch. Michelle was a pretty good cook when she was in her own element. She would ask Chemah to show her around his kitchen when he came back and she would thank him for being so nice by making him her specialty sweet potato casserole.

While waiting on the couch, Michelle heard the tumblers to the locks roll and click, but before the door even opened she heard the giggle of two voices, a boy and a girl. Michelle stiffened a little. She knew that she was going to meet Chemah's two children today, but she thought Chemah would be a buffer for their first meeting. Chemah had told her that he had explained to both of his children that morning that they would be having a visitor stay with them for a while. Chemah had told both his children at breakfast, but only Tatsuya had really been listening. Héro was oblivious when eating her Cap'n Crunch and didn't pay much attention to what Chemah said. She was only three years old and understood a lot for her age, but still, she *was* three years old. Tatsuya had perked up when he found out they were having a visitor. He wasn't especially happy about it or sad or mad, but he was very inquisitive. Tatsuya had asked his father a hundred questions about their soon-to-be visitor. And when he found out she was blind, he had another hundred questions that Chemah had no time to answer.

Michelle waited nervously for someone to notice her on the couch, but she didn't have to wait longer. Héro walked right over to her and startled her by putting the flat of her hand on her cheek. "You got a hurt," the little girl said.

Instinctively, Michelle jumped slightly, but not enough to dislodge Héro's hand from her face.

"Héro, no," Tatsuya chastised her, coming over and pulling her away. "Sorry about that, miss," Tatsuya said. He'ro pulled herself away from her brother again and started to climb on Michelle's lap.

"Oh," Michelle said, startled again.

"Héro, stop it," her older brother admonished her again. Tatsuya tried to take her off Michelle's lap, but Michelle intervened.

"It's all right," she said to Tatsuya. She was trying to gather Héro up in her arms, but Héro wasn't having it. She climbed onto Michelle's right leg on her own and then decided she was not comfortable enough and shifted over to her left leg. By the time their babysitter Patricia Richmond finished putting down her handbag and the groceries she was carrying, Héro was already playing in Michelle's hair. Tatsuya was looking on helplessly as if he were watching a trapeze artist working without a net.

Ms. Richmond was a black woman in her early fifties. She was very dark-skinned and carried herself with the dignity and aplomb of an African queen. She had raised her own children and was very proud of the job she had done, having produced a doctor, a lawyer, and a social worker. When she'd heard that her next-door neighbor was looking for someone to take care of the kids after school, she had volunteered to do it for free. Chemah insisted that she get paid, and she didn't resist. Chemah recognized her as a no-nonsense woman and thought that the children could benefit from a strong hand. She helped Tatsuya with his homework and kept He'ro out of trouble until Chemah got home from work. Chemah appreciated her immensely, as he stayed out late on cases sometimes and she never complained. The preoccupied sitter finally came over.

"Hello?" she said more as a question than a greeting.

Michelle turned her head slightly toward the voice and said "hi" with as much joy in her voice as she could muster. She knew she must look frightening with the welt that she had on her face.

"Is Mr. Rivers here?" Ms. Richmond asked Michelle.

"Yes, he's in the backyard taking care of my dog," Michelle said, still smiling.

At the mention of the word "dog," Ms. Richmond had blanched and looked around as if she were in mortal danger. Michelle hadn't seen the gesture, but it would have been obvious to anyone with sight that Ms. Richmond was not comfortable at the mention of a dog being anywhere near her. Michelle heard the back door open and the scuffle of paws and feet coming up the stairs together. She didn't know how Base would react to the children, so she shouted out to Chemah to hold onto him.

"Chemah, your kids are here," she shouted too loudly for Ms. Richmond's sensitive ears. "Grab Base."

Chemah came through the kitchen door holding Base by the collar.

When the two children saw Base they both gasped at the same time. Ms. Richmond gasped, too, but for a different reason. Héro jumped off Michelle's lap and ran toward the dog that was easily five inches taller than she was. Chemah held Base tightly by the collar, but it was unnecessary. Héro slammed into the dog's chest and forelegs at full speed with her arms wide open and embraced the dog as if he were a great, big stuffed animal. Base allowed her to hug him and stroke him until Tatsuya came over to touch him. When Tatsuya touched the top of Base's head the dog responded by nuzzling the boy in return. Chemah let go of Base's collar and watched the dog and the children get to know one another. The children were all over Base and Base seemed to be in his glory, licking at and nuzzling them back for every petting he received.

Michelle was listening intently for a sign of discontent from Base, but heard not a one. She heard Base's heavy panting and his happily wagging tail slapping the floor occasionally. It was all good until Ms. Richmond spoke.

"Mr. Rivers, can I talk to you in the kitchen a second?" the babysitter asked, taking a step toward Chemah. Base's ears pricked slightly as if he had just seen and heard her for the first time. Chemah grabbed his collar when he heard the low growl that he knew meant Base would attack. Ms. Richmond heard the growl and stopped in her tracks. She looked at the dog a moment, calculating something in her head, then stepped fearlessly past Chemah and the dog toward the kitchen.

Chemah was impressed by Ms. Richmond's fearless demeanor, but knew better than to let go of Base while she was still in the room. When Ms. Richmond reached the safety of the other room, Chemah let go of the dog again and the children resumed their petting. Chemah went into the kitchen to face the music. Ms. Richmond did not mince words.

"Mr. Rivers, I'm not one to tell you about who or what you can have in your house, but as long as you have that dog in here I'm afraid I won't be able to come into the house."

Chemah tried to apologize to this woman who had been a savior in his life. "I'm sorry about the dog, Ms. Richmond. Anytime you come over I'll have him locked up in another room or put him outside."

Ms. Richmond looked at Chemah wearily. "Boy, I am not scared of that dog," the older woman said indignantly. "I'm allergic. It wouldn't matter if you put him away when I came over, the dog hair and dander would still be in the air and I would get sick." Ms. Richmond sniffed the air. "I can feel it coming on already."

"Ms. Richmond, it's very important that I have my guests here, but it won't be for long, a few days at the most," Chemah promised.

"I guess I can keep them over my house after school for a few days. You can come pick them up when you get off work," she said, as if it were all settled.

"Thank you, Ms. Richmond. I appreciate it."

Ms. Richmond started to walk out of the kitchen and thought better of it.

She stepped to the side and let Chemah walk out first, she was brave, but she wasn't stupid. She waited a full ten seconds before she walked out of the kitchen. That would give Chemah enough time to get hold of the dog while she got her things together. When Ms. Richmond stepped out of the kitchen, what she saw made her smile. Base lay on his back next to his female master, and he was being choked by the three-year-old who thought he was her living teddy bear. Tatsuya was rubbing his stomach, causing Base to pant happily. Ms. Richmond grabbed up her belongings and headed for the door. The dog never turned his head toward her. Chemah held the door open and waved to her as she went down the walkway and two houses down to her own brownstone.

Chemah closed the front door and went into the living room to sit down next to Michelle. "So you met the kids," Chemah said to her.

Michelle smiled kindly, but didn't say anything. Chemah expected Michelle to gush over them and tell him how great his kids were, how beautiful Héro was and what a handsome young man Tatsuya was. Chemah was almost disappointed when none of those things were said. Chemah looked at Michelle and knew that although she was smiling, she was very uncomfortable. He was sorry that he hadn't been in the room when the kids came home. He didn't get a chance to properly introduce them and now the time had passed. After Michelle had asked him yesterday how he thought the kids would respond to having a new face in their house, Chemah hadn't even thought about how she would be affected. Chemah thought to ask her if she wanted to go home, but if she said yes he would have to call someone to mind the kids while he went out. *Better to give it a few days,* he thought.

"Okay, guys, what are we having for dinner?" Chemah asked standing up.

Héro immediately came to attention. "McDonald's!" she shouted.

"Uh-uh," her father said. "You don't even like hamburgers; you want the Happy Meal gift."

Héro was obstinate. "McDonald's, McDonald's," she kept repeating. She already knew how to get her father to do whatever she wanted.

"I was going to offer my services in the kitchen," Michelle said, "but it appears that we're headed to McDonald's."

"You can burn?" Chemah asked.

"Any real sister can burn," Michelle said, crossing her legs and sitting back for emphasis. "Any real sister worth a damn, anyway," she continued, folding her arms over her chest. "I couldn't always cook, though, the first time I made sweet potato casserole, I gave Base a piece and a minute later I could hear him licking his butt in an effort to get the taste out of his mouth."

Chemah laughed, but wondered if she was joking.

Héro was not getting the attention she desired and went back to petting Base.

"So you think you might want to try your hand in my kitchen?" Chemah tried to sound unenthusiastic.

Michelle could already read him. "Oh, no, brother," she said. "Don't do me any favors. I would hate to mess up your precious kitchen."

Chemah's feeble attempt at reverse psychology had not worked, so he played another hand. "Woman, you gonna let these kids starve?"

"Chemah, you have no shame," Michelle said. "You gonna use your kids to get whatever you want, huh?" Michelle stood abruptly and Chemah took her by the elbow and started to lead her to the kitchen. "You ever have sweet potato casserole?" Michelle asked.

"Aw, hell no!" Chemah said, making a disgusted face.

"I guess tonight's your lucky night."

Michelle asked Chemah for some ingredients and he jumped to get them. He would tease her about how everything had to be exact and then he'd gently hand her what she'd asked for, always finding an opportunity to brush against her. She started calling him her assistant and he didn't mind. They didn't laugh a lot, but neither of them lost the smiles on their faces. They were going to be happy all night. Right up until the time they had to talk about the case again. Then they'd both be scared.

Chapter 13
HAND TO HAND

Keith had awakened Chemah at 6:00 a.m. Chemah was groggy when he answered the phone. "Hello," he said, his voice filled with phlegm.

"Hello, Chemah?" Keith's voice seemed nervous.

Chemah recognized the voice immediately and wiped the sleep out of his eyes, trying to become alert. "What's wrong,?" Chemah asked, remembering he had told the kid to call if anything came up.

"Nothing's wrong, I was simply checking up on you. You didn't come in yesterday, and I thought you might be sick or something."

"Didn't the captain tell you that I wasn't coming in? That I had to take care of some departmental business?" Chemah said.

"No, he didn't say anything to me. I didn't see him until the end of the day," Keith explained.

"Well, when you saw him, didn't you ask him what happened to your partner?" Chemah was getting heated.

"Why should I?" Keith asked. "He already doesn't like me. The next thing you know he'll have me cleaning the toilet."

Chemah knew how the kid felt. He had gone through the same thing years ago with the captain. "Listen, Keith, I know it's hard, but you've got to stand up to the captain. You've got to let him know that you're not going to take any of his shit. Let him know you're a man, just like he is. It's the only way he'll ever give you your props. If he thinks you're afraid, he'll ride you till the wheels fall off," Chemah said. "And if you're my partner, you always have to have my back. I got your back no matter what happens."

"A lot of good that did the other day," Keith said, alluding to the ass chewing that the captain had given him for making bad decisions during the weekend.

Chemah was tired of the whining. "I'll be in a little late today, have you checked on Kelly and Fritz? They have anything new on the kid they're tailing?" Chemah asked.

"I haven't talked to them in two days," Keith answered.

Chemah was getting mad again. "You haven't talked to them in two days? Why the fuck not?"

"I told you, the captain gave me a bunch of bullshit jobs to do."

"Fuck, so you let your responsibilities for the most important case in the city go down the fucking tubes?" Chemah said, almost screaming.

"You took a day off, too." Keith said, whining again.

"I told you, I didn't take a day off, I was handling departmental business." Chemah was losing it again. Keith started to say something again, but Chemah cut him off. "Get on your job, kid, we'll talk again later. I'll be in around eleven." He hung up on Keith.

‡‡‡

Chemah got the kids ready for school and daycare and still hadn't heard Michelle stir in the room he had assigned her to. It was the room directly across from his. He justified putting her so close to him, so that he could be there if she needed anything in the middle of the night. They had stayed up late talking about the case and her attacker and he thought it would be best to let her sleep and heal. At least until he took the kids to school. By the time Chemah was ready to take them, they were waiting by the door with Base. He had to insist that Base could not travel to school with them. Héro had almost started to cry. She thought the dog would be lonely. Tatsuya had agreed until Chemah reminded them that Michelle would need him during the day to help her get around. Both the children hugged Base good-bye promising to get home real soon. Base seemed almost as sad to see them go when Chemah closed the door, leaving him behind.

###

Chemah was back an hour later and was greeted by Base at the door. The dog sat up when Chemah came through the door, but when he saw who it was, he yawned and lay back down. "It's nice to see you, too," Chemah said to him as he passed him to go into the kitchen. Chemah checked the refrigerator for something to eat and decided on the leftover sweet potato casserole from last night. He hadn't expected it to be good, but it was slammin.' Even the kids, who were very finicky eaters, had enjoyed it. Chemah took a big portion of it out of the pan with his bare hands and bit a big chunk out of it.

He started to walk up the stairs toward his bedroom to get ready for work when he heard a low humming noise coming from upstairs. *Michelle must already be up,* he thought, picturing her blow-drying her hair. He took two more large bites of the sweet potato casserole and it was gone. He rubbed his hands together to get rid of the crumbs and continued his ascent up the stairs. He decided he would take a shower, get dressed, and then talk to Michelle about how she would be spending her day.

As he passed the door to Michelle's room, he noticed that the door was slightly ajar, but it wasn't open enough to see into the entire room. He thought he saw some movement inside as he passed. Chemah got to the door to his room when he realized that the low humming that he had been hearing was not the noise that a hair dryer makes. Chemah almost ignored it, but his curiosity got the better of him and he walked back toward Michelle's door.

The closer he got to the door, the louder the humming noise became. Chemah didn't want to disturb the door, but he couldn't see entirely into the room without opening it a little. Chemah carefully applied a little pressure on the door. He only needed it to be open a fraction of an inch more so that he could see into the room. He pressed on the door again, hoping that it wouldn't squeak. Michelle had perfect hearing and he didn't want her to think he was spying on her. Luckily it didn't making a noise.

Michelle was on the bed facing directly toward Chemah with her legs wide open, knees pulled back almost to her shoulders. Her left hand was between her legs, manipulating a small vibrator that was about the size of a small Magic

Marker over her engorged and slippery-looking clitoris. If Chemah had known anything about vibrators, he would have identified it as a pocket rocket, the most powerful battery-powered vibrator you could find. Chemah started to close the door shut when he saw her staring right at him. He'd almost forgotten she was blind. Michelle's other hand was kneading her right breast. The way she was squeezing it made the nipple jut out unnaturally. Chemah bit his lip to stifle a moan from escaping his mouth when his eyes focused on the thimble-size nipples.

Chemah straightened himself slowly, determined to do the right thing, when he felt his penis push hard against his pants. He grimaced and used his right hand to push down hard on his erection in an attempt to make it go back down. The only thing he really accomplished by this gesture was to create a link between his brain and his dick that only his hand could complete. His dick was urging his brain to bring that hand back, but the brain would not comply immediately. Chemah's morals and self-discipline were momentarily winning. As Chemah started to move away from the door, Michelle decided to change positions. Her movement caught Chemah's attention and he brought his face back to the small crack in the door that would allow him to continue watching.

Michelle turned over onto her knees and then widened her stance as she leaned forward, arching her ass into the air. Michelle used one elbow to hold herself steady on the bed, while the other reached underneath her and continued to massage her clitoris with the small vibrator. From this position, Chemah could see every facet of Michelle's sexuality. He could see her breasts swing like pendulums between her legs, the nipples swelling even more as the blood flowed downward into them. Her anus stared at him, winking repeatedly as her sphincter was forced to contract through each wave of pleasure that the vibrator released in her.

Michelle's vagina was the last thing that caught Chemah's attention. It was swollen and open. The lips were not small and pouting like a young woman's might be. *That is abnormally large,* Chemah thought, never before having seen that part of a woman's anatomy reach those proportions. Michelle's orifice hung apart freely and was secreting copious amounts of fluids, and Chemah's mouth mocked it, opening in a wet oval as a drop of saliva threatened to fall from the corner of his lips. Chemah controlled the animal in him that desired to push the door in and rush to the bed to glue his mouth to her yawning pussy.

However, he was not strong enough to keep his hand from pulling down his pants zipper and reaching for his dick. Chemah's hand found his penis and he sighed with relief. It was already harder than it had ever been in the last four years and he knew a few strokes would make it go off. At first he started to stroke it furiously, craving the release from the hold that his animal nature had over him, that only an orgasm would give him freedom from. After moments of watching Michelle masturbate and stroking his penis in time with her movements, Chemah was able to catch his breath and gain control of his senses again.

As Chemah watched, Michelle let all of her upper body weight rest on one shoulder while she reached around with the hand that she freed up and inserted the middle digit into her dripping hole. Michelle cried out in ecstasy as the finger was sucked in to the third knuckle. Chemah's hand on his dick kept time with her finger as it alternately plunged in and out of her sucking hole. Chemah could hear Michelle egging herself on as she went faster and faster. Chemah couldn't tell what she was saying, but the rhythm of her chant was in time with his hand and hers. Michelle inserted a second and then a third finger next to the first and her chanting suddenly became louder. It was barely audible but it was distinct to Chemah's ear: "Fuck me, Chemah, fuck me, Chemah, fuck me, Chemah..." she was saying.

The realization of her words were enough to send Chemah over the edge. His senses were overloaded. Should he rush into the room and ram himself into her, fulfilling both of their needs? Or should he...too late, his seed was already spilling onto the floor. When he realized that he could not stop the flow of cum, he stroked himself faster in an attempt to get it all over with faster. As the cum ebbed, the guilt started to creep in. Michelle was still fucking herself furiously, with four fingers now, Chemah noticed. Chemah didn't bother putting his wet and limp member away. He wanted to get away from the scene of the crime as fast as he could. He didn't wear underwear and the residual cum would only stain his pants. Chemah took a last look into Michelle's room and then turned to walk the few steps back into his room, his dick dripping out in front of him.

Chemah decided to take another shower before going to work. His master bedroom had its own full bathroom, complete with Jacuzzi. If it were the weekend or he'd had enough time he might have opted for a long soak in the jet-enhanced tub. Not having either option, he turned the hot water on full blast and got beneath it, letting the steam and water work the residual tightness caused by his rushed orgasm out of his shoulders.

‡‡‡

After getting fully dressed again, Chemah went downstairs to the kitchen. He was always ravenous after sex and he'd thought about the sweet potato casserole the whole time he showered. Chemah pushed the door to the kitchen and it was met with resistance and an "ouch." It was Michelle. Chemah pushed the door again, but slowly this time and entered the kitchen. Michelle was standing by the table, rubbing her forehead. "I'm sorry, Michelle. I didn't know you were in here," Chemah apologized. Michelle was smiling, but she was still rubbing the pain away.

"No problem," she said. "You almost get used to the bumps and spills, but the pain…not so much."

Chemah had the urge to take her head in his hands and kiss the pain away from her forehead. He recognized the symptoms of his thinking and behavior. The last time he felt like this, he'd fought it and eventually it had caused him great anguish and the loss of a loved one. He was determined that he would not make the same mistake again.

If a great love comes once and you don't answer it, you've made a mistake, he thought. *If it comes twice and you don't answer it, you're a fool.* With that thought, Chemah walked over to Michelle, who was still rubbing her forehead, and held her head gently on either side of her temples. Michelle stood still for a moment, not sure of what to expect. Chemah planted a soft kiss onto her forehead.

Before his lips could pull away from her brow, Michelle jerked away suddenly. "What are you doing?" she said.

"I…I…I…I just thought I'd kiss the pain away," Chemah stammered.

Michelle had a frown on her face. There was an uncomfortable silence and before Chemah could speak again, Michelle said, "I don't need my pain kissed away. I may need your protection and I may even need a good fuck, but I don't need my pain kissed away."

Chemah was taken aback by the harshness of Michelle's confession. He must have misread all the signs he thought were there. For his part, he was sure that he was falling in love with this beautiful, strong, and funny woman. In his previous two relationships, the two women he thought he was in love with were so enamored with him he didn't have to do anything but let himself be loved. He had never dwelled on how it would feel to be in love with someone who didn't want him. He felt the hurt of rejection and it left a searing pain where good feelings ought to be. Michelle hadn't meant to castrate Chemah with her words, but she was tired of men taking it for granted that she was so helpless and in need of them. When she had her sight and men treated her as if she were a paper doll, she could always be counted on to set them straight. This was no different, she convinced herself. She didn't need anyone kissing away her boo-boo. She was a grown-ass woman and could do for herself. That's why she couldn't have a man in her life now. She didn't want any man who thought she needed him more than he needed her. *It's a damn shame,* she thought as the silence in the kitchen between her and Chemah became deafening.

She thought Chemah would be different. She didn't know why she had thought that. Hadn't even her father been predictable as a man? Thinking that she needed him to protect her under his roof when she became blind, and then refusing to speak to her when she didn't accept all he offered. *Fuck all of 'em,* she thought.

Michelle started to feel around the kitchen for the counter she knew would lead her to the door when she felt Chemah grab her arm. His grip was gentle but authoritative. "I didn't mean to offend you," he said. "I thought we shared the same feelings."

"And what feelings would those be?" Michelle asked. "And I dare you to say you love me. 'Cause, mister, you don't even know me."

Chemah was left with his mouth hanging open. He did love her. It was the instantaneous kind of love that he'd felt for his son's mother who had died four years ago. He didn't think he'd ever feel this way again and now that he did, he was being cowed into not saying it by a blind woman. His silence was all she needed as an answer. "That's what I thought," Michelle said, snatching her arm away from him. Chemah moved to grab her again but she had already made it out the door and back into the living room.

Michelle sat on the couch, reached for the television remote, and found it as if it were her own place. Chemah walked into the living room, ready to try again, but she was on him before he could get another word out. "And another thing, I'm helping you out by being here. I could be in my own place not having to deal with people who want to be my father. I'm only here because you said it would make it easier to catch this crazy motherfucker if I were out of sight. I'm not scared of shit. And I don't need shit." She knew she was getting carried away, but she couldn't stop herself.

Chemah tried again. "Is it so wrong to want to love a beautiful woman?" he said in his most disarming voice.

Michelle threw the final dagger. "If you wanted to love a beautiful woman, you should have come in the room and fucked her hard like she needed, instead of hiding in the hall, pulling on your own dick."

Chemah had no more words. He was ashamed of himself and of her. How could he love someone that cruel? Chemah didn't see the tears in her eyes and if he did, it probably wouldn't have mattered. He was through.

Michelle had amazed herself. How could she say things that hurtful to someone she wanted worse than she wanted her own sight? *Shit, love hurts,* she thought.

Chapter 14
Nowhere to Run

Victor knew he was being watched. His mother wouldn't go to bed until she was sure he was in for the night and there were two cops outside that had been shadowing him for the past three days. His mother had made him another of his favorite meals tonight and then came to his room to give him his dessert. He wasn't trying to resist anymore. He had to take care of her before she would leave his room. She had no problem performing sexual acts with him, but she would not sleep in the same bed with him. She thought it "unnatural" for a grown man and his mother to sleep in the same bed together. Victor had heard his mother and her friends refer to sexual acts that they heard others performed as "vile" and "unnatural." Victor wondered what his mother's church friends would say if they knew what he and she did behind closed doors.

When it had first happened between them, he had thought it was his fault. He had only been sixteen years old and his hormones were raging. She'd approached him when he was half-asleep in bed. He thought it was a dream at first, and as the intensity of the act increased, he had come fully awake. It had felt so good he couldn't stop it even if he'd wanted to. When they finished neither of them said a word to the other. His mother had simply gotten up and gone back to her room. She had visited him the next night and the next night after that. After weeks of this he had come to depend on it, like a junkie depends on heroin. He couldn't sleep on nights she didn't visit. That's when he had started going out into the night by himself.

At first, it was merely to get some night air. He never stayed in his own neighborhood; he didn't like the girls around there. The church girls that he knew and could have something in common with would not be out at the times he felt the need for female companionship. And if they were, would they be able to give him what he needed? The first time he tried to approach a girl she had laughed at him. It took him months before he tried to talk to another girl who was not in the church. He was only compelled when his mother did not feel the need to visit his room. As time passed and he got older, he started to need her less. He'd found his own purpose in the world and when he went out on his own again tonight, he knew his purpose would be fulfilled soon.

Victor dressed silently in his room. He put on a black hoody and black sweatpants he'd bought at Harlem USA brand apparel. They were not name-brand clothes. They were functional for what he intended to do tonight. He normally did not wear sneakers, but he'd picked up a pair of running shoes that were on sale when he got the sweats. He was almost caught the last time he went out. He couldn't run fast in his church shoes. He had no intention of running tonight, but who was to say what the Lord had in store for him.

After they fornicated, it usually didn't take long for his mother to fall asleep. Victor could almost set his watch by her. She didn't sleep hard, but she always slept fast. When Victor heard Reesey snoring in the next room, he didn't bother trying to go out the door of the apartment. He knew his mother would awaken at the sound of the door opening. The fire escape was the way his brother and he used to sneak out together when they were younger. Victor worked his way up the fire escape toward the roof. He could see the so-called unmarked police car waiting down below.

Five-O were always on the wrong side of shit. They thought he'd be stupid enough to walk right out of the building, but he was smarter than that. There was never an unmarked car in the neighborhood that everyone didn't know about. This one had been around for three days and it was the talk of the neighborhood. No one with warrants would come out onto that street until they were gone. Victor didn't have warrants, but he knew it was him they were looking for. They hadn't stopped him from leaving his home the past three days and he wasn't overly concerned about them now.

The moonlight made it easy for him to make his way across the rooftop of his building. There were seven consecutive buildings attached to one another; he would walk all the way to the last building before opening the roof door and going down the building steps, making his way out of the building like one of the building's residents. It was already two-thirty a.m. and there was still regular traffic coming out of the building. The police were facing the wrong way and weren't going to see him going or coming back.

‡‡‡

Victor made it to the 116th Street-Lenox Avenue train station without being stopped by anyone who knew him. There were still people on the street, but no one that would know Victor would be on the street at this time. He looked to his left and saw Central Park only six blocks away. He started walking swiftly toward the park. He felt drawn to the lights at its perimeter the way a moth was to a flame. He asked the Lord to give him a sign that he was going in the right direction to do his bidding, but today the Lord didn't answer him. He was on his own.

He was walking inside the park for five minutes and had reached the dropoff incline his brother and he would bring cardboard boxes to when it snowed. They'd called it Dead Man's Hill. Anyone who tried to go the full way down the hill when it was matted with ice was sure to wind up a dead man. His brother was the only one he had known to complete the slippery run successfully.

One white boy their age, who had told them he lived on Central Park West, had attempted the feat with a brand-new sleigh while they stood by and watched. Victor still remembered the cry of the young man when he'd veered off the hill and into a tree. The sight of the blood coming from the boy's cheek was sickening. His brother and he had walked the boy home the seven blocks, after which his mother had made him and his brother walk all the way back to the boy's home and give back the twenty dollars the boy's mom had given them as a reward.

Victor recalled the memory and knew he had more good in him to do.

Women passed him in skimpy shorts, running in the park, and he wondered how they thought they would outrun the danger they put themselves in at this hour. There were so many places in this park that he knew a woman could be easily dragged into and not seen again for days. That was what he was looking for now. If they had known that he was looking for that oh-so-secluded sweet spot, he was sure that they would run much faster than they were now.

‡‡‡

Victor left the park an hour later at a dead run. Although he was lean, he was out of shape. A cop had spotted him and had called out to him as he came out of the bushes. *If it weren't for bad luck, I wouldn't have any luck at all,* he thought as he slowed to a walk one block later, gasping for breath and clutching at the stitch in his side. The cop had stopped chasing him. He had no identification on him and that in itself was enough to have him taken in on suspicion. Luckily, the cop was in worse shape than Victor. He'd stopped after about a hundred yards of running. He had nothing to charge this character with except walking in the park at night, and that was not a crime. Besides, the guys were already ribbing him about the last guy he had chased and lost.

Victor walked back to his block and turned the corner to go into the building that he had come down from. Seventy yards away, staring right at him, was the young white cop who had questioned him at his apartment door. The cop had a bag in his hand. He'd probably gone to the all-night bodega down the block. Victor had to play it off. He couldn't go back the way that he'd come. They'd know that he'd fooled them. He was startled to see the cop, but he continued to walk toward him as if he didn't have a care in the world. Victor saw the man, more than heard him, bend toward the car window he was standing next to and talk to his partner. The driver's side door opened and the older black cop came out. He looked at Victor and smiled. Victor smiled back and kept walking toward the two men.

By the time Victor reached the parked car in front of his house, both cops were on the sidewalk blocking his path.

"Out for an evening walk?" the older police officer asked.

Victor walked right up to them without fear. "What's that?"

"I said, where the fuck you comin' from?" the black cop said. "And if you act stupid like you don' understand me jes one mo' time, I'm gonna tap your jaw, boy."

The man's anger seemed to have taken away his ability to speak proper English. As if on cue the police radio sparked to life. It was calling all available officers to the park; another body had been found. Victor had been paying as much attention to the radio as the two officers and was still listening intently when his jaw was "tapped."

‡‡‡

Victor awoke as he was being dragged from the unmarked car and into the police precinct. He tried to struggle free until he realized that his hands were cuffed behind him. The older officer had been the one who hit him, he was sure of it. The white cop still looked soft. Victor was sure he could have taken a punch from him.

The black cop pulled him upright and brought him close. "Walk or get dragged, your choice."

Victor allowed himself to be led down two halls and into a small room that housed a table and three chairs. He saw a mirror on the wall and knew it was a two-way mirror. Other cops would be joining them soon.

‡‡‡

The captain called Chemah as soon as they contacted him. Chemah tried to call Keith, but his cellphone was fucking up again. He'd call him when he got to the precinct. When Chemah reached the precinct the captain was waiting in front of the building.

"We've got him in room three waiting for you. Where's your partner?" the captain asked.

"My phone's not working again. I didn't get a chance to call him," Chemah said, not breaking stride with the captain as they walked through the precinct. Chemah began to walk toward the Homicide Detectives' room, intent on calling Keith, but the captain took him by the arm and pulled him into his office. He unintentionally slammed the door behind them as they crossed the threshold.

"What are you gonna do?" the captain asked Chemah after he blanched from the banging sound that the door had made.

Chemah had never seen the man look so nervous. "It's your call, Cap," Chemah said, watching the sweat on the captain's brow trickle down his shirt collar. The captain paced the room a few times while Chemah watched, perplexed by the man's visible discomfort.

Chemah had worked many cases with the captain but had never seen him this nervous. The captain stopped pacing momentarily and faced Chemah. "What's your gut on this, Chemah? You're the one that put the shadows on this guy. Do you think he's our man?"

The captain didn't wait for an answer, he started talking to himself. "Should've followed my own instincts. Shoulda brought him in before when we had the chance," he said as he started to pace in front of his desk again. Chemah folded his arms in front of his chest and waited for the captain to calm down. The gesture of folding his arms like that caught the captain's attention again.

"Whatta ya got?" the captain asked impatiently.

"Has the kid lawyered up yet?" Chemah asked.

The question made the captain come back to his senses. Chemah could see the character of the man he had come to respect so much return.

"He hasn't asked for one yet," the captain answered. "We've still got a chance to salvage this mess. Do you have a strategy?"

Chemah nodded. "Yeah, I have to wait for Keith to get here. Gotta keep the good cop-bad cop thing going."

"Fuck Medlin, he's nowhere to be found," the captain said.

"You're right. We've gotta go in and question this kid before he has enough time to think about a lawyer."

The captain loosened his tie and mussed his hair even more than it was. "Am I the good cop or the bad cop?"

The captain and Chemah had done this together before, but it had been a long time. Chemah didn't want to say it aloud, but he wasn't sure the captain still had the balls to get the job done. Instead of voicing his concern, Chemah turned the doorknob and started to walk out.

"You're the bad cop," Chemah said. "Watch my lead, but don't let your anger get out of control."

The captain was almost insulted. Had he ever?

‡‡‡

Two hours later, Chemah was pulling the captain out of the interview room. He and the lawyer that the kid had asked for an hour earlier had gotten into a shouting match. No good could come from it. It was the first time Chemah had left an interview room before the suspect. The lawyer and Victor would be walking out the door as soon as he could get the captain out. The captain hadn't played bad cop; he was more like really hateful, motherfucker cop. The perp had totally shut down before Chemah could get anything useful out of him. The kid asked for a lawyer and the captain had immediately gotten back into his role as the go-by-the-rules guy that Chemah knew he was sometimes.

Chemah and the captain were back in the captain's office for about ten seconds before Keith came walking in. There was an amused smirk on his face. "That didn't go well, did it?" he said.

"You saw?" Chemah asked,

"And heard," Keith answered. "I caught about thirty minutes of it."

Chemah would have preferred him quiet in the room with him, rather than behind the two way mirror. Keith knew how to be quiet, Chemah had learned, during the interview with Michelle.

The captain was in a foul mood already, and Keith only added fuel to the fire. "Where the fuck have you been, Medlin?" he rounded on Keith.

Keith seemed to have an answer already prepared. "Nobody called me. I was coming home from a club and saw the boys in blue racing into Central Park. I followed them in and found out what was going on." Keith turned to Chemah. "Why didn't you call me?" he said accusingly.

Chemah didn't want to make any excuses. He could blame the bullshit cell-phone service he had or he could blame the captain, who had told him that calling Keith could wait. The fact of the matter was that he hadn't called his partner in on the most important aspect of an investigation.

Chemah shrugged his shoulders. "My bad. Things were going on so fast I lost track of everything."

Keith had been around Chemah long enough to know that nothing got away from him. The man never forgot anything and there was always a method to his madness. If he didn't call Keith there was a reason for it. Keith knew it, but didn't push the subject.

"What are we going to do now?" Keith asked.

"Let's get to the crime scene. Who's there already?" Chemah asked the captain.

"Max and Jacobson," the captain answered. "I told them to secure the area until you got there. They were told not to touch anything."

Keith made a weird face and shook his head. "When I got there, there were cops everywhere. People were walking through, around, and past the crime scene," Keith said in disgust.

"You should've stayed and taken over the investigation," Chemah said.

The captain leered at Keith as if he were going to spit on him. Chemah recognized the expression and decided to get Keith out of there before the captain started in on him. The captain hated the younger man and Chemah knew why. It couldn't be helped. It was a changing of the guard. Out with the old and in with the new. Keith wouldn't be free of the captain's wrath until he proved he deserved to be a detective. So far he was doing a poor job. He hadn't even seen fit to take over an area that should have come under his jurisdiction the minute he realized the crime was connected to his ongoing investigation.

"I'm driving. Leave your car," Chemah said to Keith.

Keith followed Chemah out the door and they were in the car before Chemah said anything else. Chemah turned the key to his BMW X5 and the engine purred with the precision that the car was known for. He rarely used his personal car for work anymore. It brought too much attention. It was only because he had been called out of his bed that he was forced to use it now.

Keith was admiring the leather interior of the car and tried to make small talk with Chemah. "This is nice," he said, feeling the leather armrest to his left. "Must have cost you at least forty thousand," Keith estimated.

"Fifty," Chemah corrected him.

"Fifty? Damn. On our salary? I don't see it. What you got? Some side business going or something? How can you afford this on our salary?"

Chemah wasn't used to anyone coming right out and asking about his finances. He realized people wondered about how well he lived, but no one ever dared to ask. "I've made some good investments," was all he said to Keith.

Chemah had always driven a BMW, it was the first car he had ever bought with an inheritance from a dead relative, but the truth was that he received a sizable addition to his salary via child support. His ex-wife, Margarita, the mother of his daughter, Héro, had been a partner in a consulting firm and was worth millions. They had bought her out when she was sent to prison four years earlier. Part of the settlement had gone to Chemah. Margarita had insisted that her only daughter live in the comfort and style that she would have given her herself had she not been in the penitentiary. Keith didn't need to know any of this and Chemah didn't volunteer the information. They discussed the specs of the car the rest of the way to the crime scene.

When they arrived at the scene, it was as Keith had described. The crime scene was taped off, but too many people were being allowed to come and go in the area. The coroner was already there and had trampled all over everything. God knows how many other officers had come into the area to stop the newspaper photographers who were trying to get tomorrow's front-page picture. Chemah didn't have to identify himself when he came on the scene. Everyone had been waiting for him. The detectives who were holding him down the crime scene gave him a short synopsis of what they had interpreted from their findings. They never looked twice at Keith.

Chemah immediately set up a perimeter sixty yards around the body and had an officer stationed on every side to ensure that no one entered. Keith followed him around as Chemah had told him to in the car. They made a good team, Chemah thought for the second time since he'd met Keith. He allowed Keith to walk the crime scene with him and point out various evidence. He even pointed out some things Chemah might have overlooked on his first walk-through. He was taking notes and learning fast, Chemah thought. The kid was a regular Sherlock Holmes. Now all he had to do was grow a set of balls.

Chapter 15
BROOKLYN'S IN THE HOUSE

C hemah had a long day at work. The captain had to explain to his superiors why they had not been informed that there was ongoing surveillance on a suspect who now knew he was being watched. Chemah had to write a report as an addendum to the captain's report. The shit had hit the fan and he was in the thick of it. Through it all, the captain never mentioned to Chemah that he would have to inform his bosses that Chemah was harboring a witness. Both there asses would have been in a sling over this, if anyone had ever found out about it.

When he pushed the key into the lock, the door creaked open, offering no resistance. Chemah was instantly on alert. He remembered that his children were safe at his neighbor's house and the thought stopped him from running headlong into a potentially dangerous situation. Chemah pulled the semiautomatic Smith and Wesson firearm out of the holster at his side and slowly pushed the door the rest of the way open. He looked into the full length of the living room and could see nothing out of place. He ducked his face quickly in and then out of the room in an attempt to see and draw fire from anyone waiting right inside the doorway.

He made the movement to the left and then to the right. When nothing happened he stepped quietly through the door. He moved slowly along the wall of the living room, stepping as nimbly as Usher in a music video. Chemah stopped at the staircase and listened for any sound coming from upstairs. As he began to ascend the staircase, he heard a sound from the kitchen. He came back down the three steps he had taken twice as fast as he had gone up. Chemah moved quickly toward the kitchen door and pushed it open with his gun extended in front of him. There was no one in the kitchen, but Chemah could hear the voices of his children coming from the back door that led from the kitchen to the yard. Chemah blew out an exasperated breath and put his gun away.

He looked out the half-open door and was surprised at what he saw in his backyard. Héro and Tatsuya were turning two ropes Double Dutch style and Michelle was in the middle of the ropes jumping. She wasn't merely jumping, she was doing tricks. Michelle's feet moved twice as fast as the rope. She turned, touched the ground, jumped quickly to her feet, and then hopped on one leg as she turned again. Chemah came all the way through the door.

As it banged closed behind him, the children stopped turning the rope and looked up the stairs that led up to the deck Chemah stood on. The two children simultaneously dropped the rope ends they were holding, leaving Michelle in a tangle of rope. They ran up the steps to their father, Tatsuya reaching him first and jumping into his arms the way he had since they had first met four years ago. Chemah thought he was getting kind of big to being doing that, but refused to discourage Tatsuya from showing affection. Chemah held him tightly until he heard his daughter scream up at him. "DADDYYYY!!!" she yelled, trying to pull herself up by his pants leg. Chemah shifted Tatsuya to one arm and reached down to pick his daughter up. He lifted her easily and held both his children to his chest.

Chemah looked down into his yard at Michelle, who had disentangled herself from the rope the children had discarded upon their father's arrival. She stood in the middle of the yard, not moving. Base looked up from where he lay in a corner. He looked at Chemah, then at his master, and decided that he was not needed yet. He put his head back down against his paws, but kept his eyes on Michelle.

Chemah walked down the steps with the two children still in his arms. He hadn't exactly made peace with Michelle in the two weeks that she had been in the house. She had deliberately humiliated him and said things that were hurtful when he had made it clear that he had feelings for her. Chemah was finding it hard to forgive her trespasses.

Alternately, on a daily basis Michelle did or said something that made Chemah want to tell her how perfect she was for him. She was funny and smart and her disability did not seem to affect her negatively in any way, except she couldn't be as mobile as she would have wanted to be. Chemah reached the bottom of the steps and couldn't help smiling as he addressed her. He was still holding a child in each arm when he said, "That was pretty good."

Michelle's face relaxed into a smug smile, not realizing that Chemah had paused for effect. "That is, pretty good for a Brooklyn girl," Chemah continued. "Of course, everybody knows Harlem always had the best Double Dutch jumpers."

The remark didn't faze Michelle; she knew Chemah was trying to play her and she was too cool to bite the bait. She bit her lip and appeared to be contemplating something for a moment before she said, " Hmm, you may be right about that, those Harlem girls always did spread their legs wider when they did a split," and then Michelle mimicked Chemah's tactic of pausing for effect. For Chemah, the three seconds that passed were like watching a slow-motion slap from your grandmother that you couldn't block. Then she finally said it. "But you damn sure couldn't beat us at skellies." Chemah almost dropped the kids. He put them down quickly and walked around Michelle talking loudly in a high pitched voice that was almost unrecognizable as his own, "Oh hell no, you didn't say Brooklyn could beat Harlem at skellies. We invented skellies in Harlem." Chemah was going off for a full twenty seconds before he noticed his kids were staring up at him.

Chemah was usually the perfect example of decorum during any excitable situation. The children had never seen their father rant on like this before. They weren't scared, they found it just as amusing as Michelle, who now had a look of complete satisfaction on her face. Chemah smiled when he realized how much he had gone on about the subject of skellies, and he was acknowledging to himself how easily Michelle pushed his buttons when Tatsuya asked, "What's skellies?"

Michelle was incredulous as she turned to Chemah. "This boy's nine years old, living in Harlem, and he doesn't know what skellies is! Where have you been hiding him? That's why the boy is having problems in school now, you never let him go out of the house alone. Always protecting somebody; like they need protecting." Chemah looked sheepish as Michelle continued to rant on about Tatsuya's lack of street culture.

He acted as if he were not listening when in fact he heard it all. He heard Michelle project her feelings about how Chemah overprotected her through her tirade about Tatsuya, but he also heard some wisdom in how he should allow the boy to socialize in the neighborhood without the benefit of parental supervision. Michelle had a big goddamn mouth, but she was right. It was time to let Tatsuya do some things on his own. There are some tough kids in Harlem's streets, but the streets were still a testing ground for life. Chemah still recognized this as a place where he built some of his character. Maybe if he'd let Tatsuya play with some of the neighborhood kids earlier, he wouldn't be having the problems he was having with those bourgeois kids in the private school he attended. There was no use in lamenting over it anymore, he thought. First things first, teach the kid to play some skellies.

"Tatsuya, go up to your room and get some chalk out of your crayon box."

Tatsuya dashed off without asking another question. Before he reached the top of the deck stairs, Chemah called after him again. "Tatsuya, on your way back down, go into the refrigerator and take the caps off the gallon of milk and the sixty-four-ounce soda bottle and bring them back with you."

Tatsuya gave Chemah a twisted look until Chemah said, "Do what I tell you. I'll show you what we're going to do when you get back."

Tatsuya took off again and Chemah saw his daughter pick up the Double Dutch ropes and try to turn them on her own with no one on the other side. One of the ropes struck Michelle on the leg, making her wince unexpectedly. After a quick try, she looked at her father and said, "Turn, Daddy. Turn the rope."

Chemah walked over to the opposite side of his daughter and picked up the limp rope.

Instead of turning them, he brought them forward to where Michelle stood. "Here, you turn," he said to Michelle, putting the rope in her hands.

"You're gonna jump?" Michelle asked, patronizing Chemah.

"That's right. I'm gonna jump. Why? Are you saying boys can't jump?" Chemah asked.

"Oh no. I'm not saying boys can't jump," Michelle answered. "But in my neighborhood, any boy that could jump really well, was usually a, you know…" Michelle raised her right hand and let it hang limply at the wrist. Chemah refused to dignify Michelle's insinuation with a response and Michelle took his silence as a sign that he did not understand what she was implying. "A rump ranger, a pillow biter, a cucumber kisser."

"I get it, I get it," Chemah said, trying to stop her from going on.

"Cucumber kisser," Héro mimicked Michelle. "Cucumber kisser," she repeated, liking the sound of it and giggling behind her little hand.

"See what you've done," Chemah said to Michelle, his stern glare all but impotent to Michelle, who had no sight to avert from his.

Michelle dropped the rope and held out her arms to Héro. "Come here, baby girl," she said to the little girl whose light brown hair was twisted into two plaits. The little girl came easily into Michelle's waiting arms as Michelle bent low to scoop her up. Michelle whispered something into her ear that Chemah couldn't hear and the girl giggled and whispered back into Michelle's ear. Michelle's mouth pouted at whatever the girl had whispered and she pulled her head away from their conspiratorial huddle to shake her head no. "Uh, uh, uh," Michelle said in a reproachful manner.

The little girl looked sad for a moment and then Michelle brought their heads together again for another huddle. They were whispering again and Chemah still couldn't hear what was being said. After a series of giggles and whispers between Michelle and Héro, Michelle put Héro down.

Héro walked over to her father and said, "Sorry, Daddy, I won't say that grown-up thing again." She reached up for her father and Chemah obligingly leaned down for a big wet kiss on his forehead, which he knew was her favorite spot.

Before Héro could let go of her father's neck, Michelle said, "Now go upstairs and wash your hands so that I can do your hair properly before we have dinner. Feels like Buckwheat was the last person to do your hair."

"But I want to see skellie," Héro whined softly, looking up at her father.

Chemah was about to bend down and pick his daughter up when Michelle said in a very formidable voice "Don't look at your father, you heard what I said. Go upstairs and wash your hands."

Chemah looked sharply at Michelle, who was not even facing in their direction, but before he could contradict her, Héro had stamped off up the deck stairs heading for her room.

"I swear, you and Tatsuya let that girl get away with murder." Michelle turned her head in Chemah's general direction. Chemah didn't like anyone interfering with his children, but he knew Michelle was right. He thought he had a pretty good handle on how to deal with his son, remembering what felt good and what he felt was unnecessary when he was growing up, but Héro was a different story. He didn't have a clue where to begin and where to end in the disciplining of a girl department. Generally speaking, she was a very good child, but there were moments when she was very willful and at those times he always succumbed to her latest desire. There was a brief moment when he felt Michelle was overstepping her bounds and encroaching on his duties as a father, but he fast realized that he would have handled the situation wrong, given the opportunity.

Chemah had recently fantasized about a life with Michelle. His living experience with his ex-wife, Margarita, had been no picnic. The only thing the same about the two women was that they made things they wanted to happen. Margarita never raised her voice the way Michelle did. She had made things happen by simply lying, manipulating, and softly threatening in a way that sent icy chills up your ass. Michelle, on the other hand, had no qualms about raising her voice and demanding you do things when and how she wanted. There was honesty in her method, he thought, but still, sometimes it fucked with his nerves.

Chemah felt another tirade about to come from Michelle and thought it was about time he answered to her earlier accusations of his overprotection. "How do you feel about going back to Caroline's? If you could get a gig there?" Chemah asked.

Michelle's mouth had been open and in the middle of creating a vowel when she heard Chemah's question. Michelle swallowed the word and attitude she was about to give Chemah, but she didn't want to take more than a moment to answer him, lest he change his mind. She had grown very fond of the children and had involved herself deeply in their everyday lives in the past three weeks. But the only chance that she'd had to leave the house was to pick the children up from school with the woman from next door who normally took care of them.

After three weeks of spending time with them, today Michelle had assured Ms. Richmond that she could take care of the children herself when the elder woman had taken sick with a stomach virus. Now she was restraining herself from seeming too anxious to get away from them. "I can call my friend Rhonda and see if she can fit me into the lineup tomorrow night," she said offhandedly.

"I was thinking more like the weekend," Chemah answered back, a little too glib for Michelle.

She gave his cocky attitude a pass and contended with what he was offering instead. "On weekends they have their big headliner shows. I'm not sure they'll book me on such short notice," she thought out loud.

"Not to worry," Chemah said. "I went there this afternoon, thinking maybe I should check to see how tight their security is before I suggest to you that it would be all right for you to go back to work. While I was there I met your girl Rhonda, I didn't want to give her too much information about what you were doing now, but I alluded to you coming back to do a show this weekend and she said all you have to do is give her a call. She thought maybe I was your man, but I told her we were family friends. She was really concerned about you. We sat down for a while in the club and talked. She bought me lunch."

Michelle stopped listening to him. She was trying to contain the anger she was feeling. The thought that he had almost secured a gig for her without her knowledge was almost enough to take her over the edge, but the anger that was kicking her in the ass came from the thought of Rhonda and Chemah having lunch. She knew Rhonda's style. She was the female version of a player; Knockit, shopit, then stopit was her credo. She and Michelle had been friends before Michelle had become completely blind. Back in the day when they did the club scene together, people had called them sugar and spice. Rhonda's dark chocolate contrast to her pecan was always an attraction for the fantasy of a threesome.

Men who wanted to be known as ballers took them on shopping sprees and spent astronomical amounts of money on them. She and Rhonda were no fools. Early on they had made a plan. Any money they got as a gift they invested and parlayed into more money. If a gift was offered, they always opted for something that would increase in value. That was how she had accumulated such an illustrious art collection. They never accepted clothing shopping sprees, as they didn't want their attention to men to be misconstrued as an easy buy. In the end it could never be said that either of the women ever had sex for money. They never fucked anyone they didn't genuinely find attractive, and they never fulfilled any man's fantasy of the pecan-and-chocolate threesome.

Michelle had made a name for herself in the comedy industry and Rhonda rode on Michelle's wave, first as her manager and later as a promoter for comedy shows. The club scene got played out, but Michelle and Rhonda were always tight, always best friends. It wasn't until Michelle had lost her sight that their relationship had changed. Rhonda was always still down with her, but Michelle didn't want to be a third wheel on anyone's ride and refused any suggestions that they should still hang. Michelle never considered herself a hater and remembered how she and Rhonda had been given dirty looks by jealous women. At those times, they would grab their crotches in ridicule of men they had considered to be fake ballers. They would stare the women straight in the face as they exchanged high-fives and quoted, "Hate the game, not the player" in unison.

‡‡‡

Michelle could see the writing on the wall already. It was part of the game they had always played. The lunch Rhonda had paid for was an investment on money she anticipated Chemah would spend on her. All ballers felt the need to reciprocate any money spent on them multiplied by ten. She knew Rhonda had an eye for fine things and according to knowledge Michelle had garnered from Ms. Richmond, who had collected his dry cleaning on several occasions, Chemah wore nothing but the best, from Armani to Ferragamo. If he'd had his car keys in his hand Michelle knew that Rhonda would have spotted the BMW keys. It was par for the course. Add to that Chemah's genuine good nature, good looks, and fine body and Rhonda might decide this was the one they always talked about, the whole package, the one that would not get away, marriage material.

Although Michelle held no false hopes that Chemah would want her for anything more than a good fuck, she knew it would eat a hole in her soul to know that her best friend in the world had gotten with him. She checked her temper and listened to the end of what Chemah was saying. "…so while you're on the stage I can stand in the rear by the exit and see you and everyone else in the audience. What do you think?"

Michelle heard Tatsuya coming down the stairs and was glad she had a good hold on her temper. There was no telling what she would have said, given all the things he had hit her with. "I think it's a good idea," was all she said. "But let's talk about it more after dinner and the kids are in bed." Michelle signaled to Base and he came immediately to her side, then she Michelle started up the stairs and listened to Chemah commend Tatsuya on his choice of skelly tops. It was best not to berate him too much in front of the kids, Michelle thought, as she went through the sliding door.

It was odd to her that a man who was so intuitive about everything else could know so little about what would send an independent woman through the roof. She wondered what kind of woman his ex-wife was. She was probably very dependent on him, she wrongly assumed. As Michelle stepped through the door of the kitchen, Héro ran into her thighs, probably at the top speed she could muster with her little legs. Michelle blindly felt for the little girl and helped her up. "And where do you think you're going in such a rush, young lady?"

In answer, the little girl splayed her hands out in front of her to show that she had washed them.

"Did you wash your hands like I asked you to?" Michelle asked.

The little girl nodded.

"Don't nod, that's why God blessed you with a voice. Now, speak up."

"Yes," the little girl said.

"Yes what?" Michelle asked, hands on her hips.

"Yes, my hands are clean," Héro said, still holding her hands up for Michelle to see.

"Let me see," Michelle said, reaching out for the girl's hands. Michelle found the little hands with no effort as Héro willingly placed them willingly in her path.

Michelle's hands glided over the child's palms and then the back of her hands. "Very good," she said, a triumphant smile playing over her face. She had taken a stool to the upstairs bathroom and taught the little girl to wash her own hands two days earlier. Michelle was pleased with what her effort had produced.

"Do you know where your comb and brush are?" Michelle asked Héro. The little girl nodded and Michelle expectantly crossed her arms over her chest and waited for a proper answer. Little Héro looked up at Michelle just as expectantly and it was a few moments before it dawned on the bright little girl what was expected of her. In her realization, the little girl's mouth popped into a tight little O. The flat of her hand came up to her mouth quickly as if she had already said something she wasn't supposed to. She put her hand back down at her side as quickly as it had touched the edges of her lips.

"The comb's upstairs," she said, pointing to the staircase.

"Go upstairs and get it and come back downstairs, I want to listen to the news while I do your hair," Michelle told her.

Héro stomped her foot and didn't move. She was determined to watch this new "skelly" game that she had heard her father talk about.

Michelle was through. She was not having a three-year-old girl tell her what she was and was not going to do. Her voice raised about five octaves. "Girl, did you hear what I said? I'm *not* your father. I will tear your little ass *up*. If you don't hurry your little tail…"

The rest of the words were lost on Héro. She had taken off up the stairs like the devil was behind her as Michelle's words trailed behind her. "You gonna stand there like I won't slap fire out your little ass. You go right ahead and try me if you want to…"

Chemah was on his knees drawing Tatsuya a skelly board on the ground, when he heard Michelle start yelling. It was the first time he had heard her raise her voice to either of the children. His first instinct was to get up and stop Michelle, but on second thought, he believed her bark was worse than her bite. He was sure she meant every word that she said, but he knew there was no maliciousness in her. Ms. Richmond always said to him, "It takes a village to raise a child," and he decided she was right. Thank God Héro's mother wasn't around to hear it, he thought. She would've been all over Michelle like pimples on a fat woman's buttocks. Chemah looked up from the board he was drawing on the ground. He knew it was Michelle up in the house yelling, but for a moment he could have sworn it was his own mother.

Chapter 16
A Party Ain't a Party

ifty Cent was pumping through the apartment. The bass coming out of the speakers was virtually making the walls shake with every staccato beat of the song that reverberated into it. Victor had been invited to a house party in his building by Jeffrey Lawrence (Big Jeff), one of his childhood friends. He hadn't hung out with Jeff since they had gone to separate high schools. They always saw each other in the building and sometimes even stopped to shoot the shit. Jeff was popular in the neighborhood because he threw parties in his apartment once a month. Although Jeff wasn't a church boy like Victor, when his mother had found out that she had terminal cancer, she had gone to church with Victor and his mother quite often. Now that she was dead, Jeff threw parties once a month in the apartment to supplement the meager income that he made as an assistant manager at McDonald's. Yesterday, when he invited Victor to the party, he had explained that he planned to use the money that he made from the parties to pay tuition. He wanted to go back to school as he'd had to quit Borough of Manhattan Community College to help support the house when his mother had first become ill.

Initially, Victor had declined the invitation. He had found his purpose outside of the neighborhood and didn't want to think of what would happen if anyone thought that he was the one the police were waiting for every day outside the building. That was the deciding factor for him. It was the second Friday of the month and according to the schedule he knew he was keeping, he would be due to go out again tonight. Victor knew he should be out of the neighborhood, but maybe if he didn't go, the police would finally leave him alone. According to schedule, they knew he was due to be out of the neighborhood tonight. No matter what it cost him in sleep tonight, he would not leave the building, he promised himself.

‡‡‡

Mrs. Brown had taken to an occasional drink since Victor began locking his bedroom door every night before going to bed. She asked him every morning how he'd slept and his answer was always, "Just fine." Her drinking was usually under control, but Victor noticed that on Friday nights she drank a little more than usual. He expected that she would be drinking tonight and he didn't know if he should be in the apartment with her while she was inebriated. When Jeff told Victor that some of their old junior high school friends would also be at the party, he decided that having a reunion wouldn't be that bad.

The party spilled out of the apartment and into the hallway. Most of the tenants in the building knew what the parties were for and didn't complain, even if they didn't participate. Victor was having fun without even trying. He couldn't go near the living room, which acted as a dance floor, without people pulling him in and grinding their bodies against his to the beat of whatever happened to be playing. He'd already danced with three different young women since he'd come in an hour before. He was on the dance floor, holding on to the hips of a slightly overweight young lady with a pretty face, when Jeff saw him and frantically waved for him to come over. Victor pointed down at the woman, who had her backside glued to his groin, hoping that Jeff got the message. But Jeff made a face and waved even more forcefully before ducking outside the doorway for a second and reappearing with another brother standing next to him.

Jeff waved again and this time pointed to the brother who had come to the doorway with him. Victor's eyes had adjusted to the dark a long time before, but he could still not believe his eyes. It was Franklyn Jackson. His old best friend from junior high school. Victor disengaged himself from the waist of the woman in front of him, but the girl didn't miss a beat. She spun, rocked her hips, and gyrated a few feet before she found her next dance partner.

Victor made his way to the doorway that Jeff and Franklyn had disappeared through and had only just passed through it himself when he saw the group of boys that eleven years ago had called themselves the Fabulous Five. He wasn't part of the group himself, but they had let him and Franklyn tag along every once in a while because their mothers sometimes made their older brothers responsible for them.

The Five all saw him at the same time, but it was Franklyn who looked the happiest to see him.

"Damn, son, it's been a long time," Franklyn said, giving Victor a man hug before stepping back and letting the rest of the old crew step up and give him dap or some other form of showing love. They all seemed genuinely glad to see Victor and he in turn felt like maybe he was a part of something other than what his life had turned into in the last four years.

The old crew reminisced for what seemed like hours with the only damper on Victor's night being when they asked him the whereabouts of his brother. He couldn't bring himself to answer them and by the time he almost did, Jeff, who knew his family's history, had thankfully changed the topic of conversation.

The night wore on and the party kept getting better. Victor was not a drinker, but at some point in the night someone had put a half glass of Hennessy in his hand and he did not decline it. The drink was stiff, but satisfying.

It was two in the morning and the party showed no signs of letting up when a tall, light-skinned and well-dressed brother came into the kitchen smiling from ear to ear. He came in adjusting his clothes and announced that he needed a good drink. After leaning over the table where the fellas were drinking to reach for a cup and pouring himself a stiff drink, the light-skinned man conspiratorially told the crew what he had been up to. The boys weren't listening at first but as he talked the story started getting interesting.

"Yeah, yeah, so I talked this fine honey into coming upstairs to the roof, you know, 'cause it's too crowded to dance down here an' shit. So she stuttering like she don't want to go, but when she sees the bottle of wine in my hand, she says, 'Yes, I'll have a drink with you.' Like she's some kind of high-class bitch an' shit. Anyway, my partners see me make my move an' shit, 'cause you know they know how I do, an' they follow us upstairs. Man, after two drinks, this bitch is all over me and my boys. Now I didn't think she would do it and all 'cause the bitch was so fine, but I said, Fuck it, I'm goin' for mine, so I tell her to, you know, give me a little special attention." The tall light-skinned man grabbed his crotch for emphasis. "Yo, this bitch went to town. She sucked my dick so hard, my eardrums popped."

Franklyn's brother was always one of the leaders of the crew and after all their years apart still took it upon himself to speak the sentiments of the group. "Man, you bullshittin'," he said, turning his chair away from the storyteller. The light-skinned man almost dropped the drink he was holding, but caught it and righted himself without spilling a drop of alcohol. "Motherfucker, you calling me a liar?" the light-skinned man said, turning back and forth in pretense of looking for a place to put his drink down.

Franklyn's brother turned his head around just enough to see Lightskin out the corner of his eye. "Motherfucker, did I stutter?" Franklyn's brother asked. Lightskin took a step toward Franklyn's brother and the rest of the Fab Five plus two closed their ranks around Lightskin before he could take a second step.

Lightskin looked around at the other seven faces around him and thought twice about taking another step. Instead, Lightskin popped the collar of his shirt in grand fashion and said, "It ain't nothing, fuck y'all if you don't believe me. I was gonna tell y'all to come back up to the roof with me. My boys are still upstairs runnin' a train on her, the long line F train. I only got one nut, you niggas could of went behind me, but fuck y'all now."

Franklyn's brother turned all the way around in his chair and faced Lightskin. "You sayin' she's still upstairs?" he asked. Lightskin didn't answer; he sneered, gave Franklyn's brother the finger, and then turned around and walked out the door. The Fab Five plus two all looked around at each for a long moment and then almost simultaneously laughed as they jostled one another to get to the door.

When Franklyn got to the door he noticed that Victor was not following the crew. He let two of the five past him and he came back into the room to get Victor. "You comin', Vic?" he asked.

"Nah, son, go 'head without me, that ain't my thing," he said in a slang that he could only mimic, as it did not flow naturally.

"Still churchin' it, huh?" Franklyn stated more than asked.

"It ain't about the church," Victor half lied.

"It's not? Come on then. We don't have to do anything. We're just going to see if he was lying. You don't think the Fab Five get down like that, do you?"

The Hennessy Victor had been sipping got the best of him. He was happy to see his childhood friend and didn't want to be a wet blanket.

Franklyn put an arm around Victor and walked him to the door. "Just like back in the day, man, we stay bringin' up the rear."

The roof was dimly lit, but Victor could see two distinct groups of people on the far side of the rooftop. They were standing approximately ten feet apart. One group was partially covering the other from Victor's view. As he and Franklyn walked closer, Victor could distinguish the Fab Five from the other group, who he could now see were lined up three deep behind the two men who were handling a woman in between them. There were six of them in all, counting Lightskin, who stood between the line and the Fab Five. Victor and Franklyn reached their small group of friends and took up space at the rear of the group. Just as when they were kids, they had to painfully crane their necks to see in between the space left by their huddled friends. The poor lighting on the roof made it doubly hard to see. There was no moon out and the night clouds cast a dark shadow over them.

‡‡‡

The woman between the two men was bent over at the waist. Her legs were spread and slightly bent. Who knew whether they were spread that wide for better balance or for easier access? Victor guessed both; the way she was rocking back and forth to meet the thrusts of the man behind her created a natural albeit animalistic vision. A cloud shifted above them and it afforded Victor a view of the woman's vulva being pulled out and stretched by the huge penis invading her on every backstroke.

Victor could barely see the man's face, but it was evident by the grip that he had on her hips that he was not apt to let go anytime soon. Before the inward stroke, he was dragging his penis a full nine inches out of her, the lips of her pussy seeming to beg the shaft not to go, finally only clutching the engorged blunt head, before once again being forced painfully back into her body. The man was using every inch to impale her onto himself and in doing so he forced her head forward so that she took the penis in her mouth farther and farther down her throat.

Victor couldn't see her face clearly, but he could see that on every inward thrust of the man behind her, her nose touched the stomach of the man in front of her. He heard low mewling and gagging noises with each thrust and it started to make his dick hard. He hoped he wasn't the only one being affected by the scene in front of him. Being behind his boys, he couldn't tell if they had hard-ons.

No one was commenting on the sight in front of them, as if it were a dream from which nobody wanted to be awoken. Victor chanced a look at the men in front of him, who were in line for their turn, and almost laughed. The man who was next in line to get to the woman's ass was biting his lip to distract himself from the tent that was threatening to become a hole in his pants. Every twenty seconds or so he would pat the tent, as if it were a pet, and mumbled some words, as if coaxing it to stay calm. The man behind him was being reckless with his dick. He had his pants and underwear bunched around his knees and was stroking his penis unashamedly while looking over the shoulder of the man in front of him. *They're either really good friends or that dude doesn't know that there's a man behind him stroking his dick,* Victor thought.

The recklessness of stroking your dick openly behind another man would be unimaginable otherwise. They were still in Harlem, after all, and even under these circumstances that action would call for a beatdown. The last man on the line looked bored and held his pants at the crotch in a thuglike manner. Victor couldn't see any discernable bulge in his pants and thought the man must be purposely ignoring the sex scene in front of him. *That was smart,* Victor thought, as he himself felt he might be coming in his pants.

Victor had not had sex nor taken care of himself in at least four weeks. The

Henny was weakening his fortitude. For a moment, he thought, if the rest of the Fab Five decided to take a turn, then he would, too. After a moment the man getting his dick sucked started to shake and made a long drawn-out, convulsing sound as he sprayed down the woman's throat. "Uuuuuuuuuggghhh-hhhhhh," he grunted, holding the woman's head in place with two hands. The woman's face was pressed into his abdomen the whole time, but she never resisted. When he was finished cumming, the man pulled his wet, limp penis out of her mouth and stepped away from the scene, a smile plastered on his face. Apparently, the penis in her mouth had a lot to do with the muffling of any sound coming from the woman, because from the moment that there was no penis in her mouth you could hear the effect that the pounding she was taking from behind was having on her. "Ugh, ugh, ugh, ugh, ugh, uuuuuuu-uuuugh," she grunted through one particularly vicious stroke. "Some, ugh, body, ugh, put, ugh, another, ugh, dick in ugh, mmmmy, mmmmmouth," she said in a raspy voice.

The next man quickly pulled his zipper down and reached into his pants for his cock. He, unlike the man behind him, was aware of the vague etiquette involved in running a train, that men should be sure that another man's penis is clear of his path, lest he start a sword fight. Now that his path was clear, he came rushing in, cock in hand. He positioned himself in front of her and was savoring the act of inserting himself into her drooling slack-jawed face so much that he never saw the punch coming.

Victor had pushed through his friends and attacked the man who was about to get his dick sucked. When the man succumbed to darkness, Victor turned his attention to the man who was still humping behind the oversexed woman. The man had barely missed a stroke, even after he saw Victor attack his boy. Victor was already on top of him and attempting to strangle him before anyone could react to his rampage. The four remaining men who were running the train, jumped him before the Fab Five could react.

Franklyn and his brother were the next to jump into the fray and moments later the other four helped to peel the men off Victor. When he finally reached Victor, Franklyn could see that the man whom Victor was strangling was staring up at Victor with only the whites of his eyes. "What the fuck?" Franklyn said, tearing at Victor's hands with his own.

A moment later, Franklyn managed to pry Victor's hands off the man's throat. When he let go, the man inhaled deeply and then choked on the oxygen of which he had been deprived.

Franklyn held onto Victor, who was still trying to get past him and get at the man who was gasping for breath right next to them. "Easy, man, easy," Franklyn said, struggling to hold Victor by his shirt front. When Victor refused to calm down and started flailing his arms at Franklyn, Franklyn let go of his shirt front and got Victor in a headlock.

"What the fuck is wrong with you, man?" he shouted into Victor's ear. "What the fuck is it?"

Victor could barely hear his boy, the chokehold Franklyn had him in was making the blood pound in his ears. Victor felt a velvety darkness envelop him, but before he let himself be absorbed into it, he spoke. With the lack of oxygen he was experiencing it came out very low, but Franklyn, who had his head pressed tightly against Victor's head, heard it clearly.

"It's my mother," Victor said in a whisper, then went limp.

Chapter 17

She Got Jokes

hemah was pacing backstage at the comedy club. Michelle was on the stage doing her routine and he was trying to keep an eye on her and the rest of the club while his mind was on a personal problem that had developed right before he'd left the house. He had gotten a call right before he and Michelle left the house, from his ex-wife, Margarita.

Margarita was out of the penitentiary. She said she wanted to come over and see Héro. Chemah had wanted to know how the hell she had gotten out so quickly. She wasn't supposed to be up for parole for another two years.

Margarita didn't even try to put shade on her manipulation of the system. "You're a big boy, Chemah. You know how the world works," Margarita said, almost taunting him. "There are still a few important people out here that owe me favors."

"You mean there's at least one more scum-sucking politician whose dirty little secrets you know, who doesn't want them known by anyone else," Chemah said accusingly.

Margarita breathed deeply through the phone as if bored by his words. "I don't want to argue with you, Chemah," she said. "I want to come over to see my little girl. You know I have every right to see her. My lawyer made sure that all my visiting rights were clear while I was incarcerated," Margarita reminded Chemah.

"The terms of the agreement were that I bring her to visit you, at least once a month, and that we share custody when you got out of jail. It doesn't say anywhere in the agreement that I have to allow you into my house to see her," Chemah almost shouted into the phone.

"Your house?" Margarita raised her voice into the receiver. "I bought that house before I even knew you, Chemah," she shouted.

"That's right, you bought the house. But you also relinquished it as part of the agreement, so unless you want to get arrested, I'd better not see your ass anywhere near the house," Chemah said, abruptly pushing the off button on the phone.

Feeling a dissatisfaction that fifteen years ago would have been quelled by the physical release slamming the phone down on the receiver gives you, Chemah reared back, ready to throw the phone at the wall, when he'd heard Michelle coming down the stairs. He didn't want Michelle to think he didn't have control of the situation and decided instead to toss the phone onto one of the pillows of the living room couch. He knew it was a bad idea, but couldn't think of anything else to prolong the inevitable conversation with his ex-wife and her lawyers. Chemah casually walked over to the wall outlet and unplugged the phone.

Margarita wasn't going to take no for an answer when it came to addressing issues pertaining to her daughter. Of that, Chemah was certain. He only hoped that he could cut a deal with Margarita before she or he did anything rash. Taking away their only line of communication was the best way he could stop her for now, but soon, she would do whatever she felt she had to do to get her way.

Margarita was only thinking about herself and their daughter. He, however, had to consider how Tatsuya would feel if he had to see the woman who had been accused of killing his mother, as well as making sure that Héro was not adversely affected by having Margarita suddenly thrust into her life on a more permanent basis.

Watching Michelle make her way down the steps earlier that night had also made him aware that his reasons for not wanting to disrupt the household were not purely unselfish. He was enjoying the role that Michelle had been slowly taking on in the few weeks that she was a guest in his household. The undercurrent of sexual tension that he and Michelle had not consummated was dizzying to say the least, but to an even greater extent, he was enjoying the effect that she was having on the children. They were both getting used to having her around.

She had pushed Tatsuya to go outside and meet new friends in their neighborhood, which was something that Chemah had been reluctant to force him into. It had worked out well, with Tatsuya making friends with a couple of boys down the street. Héro was just now getting used to following Michelle's orders without looking to Tatsuya or her father to come to her rescue. Chemah knew it was the discipline the little girl needed, but given the circumstances of not having a mother around, he could never bring himself to be the one to deny her any of her heart's desires. Chemah knew that his weakness was detrimental to his little girl's upbringing.

He was working hard to solve the murder case that had forced him to bring Michelle to his house, but knew that even if he did not solve it soon, he would have to let her go back to living her own life. Taking her to the comedy club tonight so that she could do her standup act was the first step to getting her back to her normal life. He had done everything he could thus far to prevent anything from happening to her and she was going stir crazy because of it.

Fits of laughter from the crowd were distracting him from his self-appointed assignment of scrutinizing everyone in the club from his vantage point in the wings of the stage. He hadn't been listening to Michelle's material for the first ten minutes, but the people were laughing so hard it made him listen more closely to what Michelle was saying.

"To be honest with you all, when I first went blind, the biggest problem I had was figurin' out when to stop wiping my ass (loud laughter).

Don't misunderstand me. I'm not telling you all this so that you people feel sorry for me, it just is what it is.

Unlike most people, I have to listen carefully, because that's all I got. You know, people tend to misunderstand what other people are trying to communicate, and we really misunderstand the disabled more than any other people, especially when all we have to go by is our sight. I remember when I left the doctor's office after finding out that I was losing my sight, I was so depressed I went to the Brooklyn Bridge and I was standing on a railing, thinking about jumping off. I happened to look down and see a little man with no arms dancing all around on the river-bank. I thought to myself, Life isn't so bad after all, and I climbed down from the railing. So I walked down to the riverbank to thank the little man for saving my life. I said, 'I was going to jump off that bridge and kill myself, but when I saw you dancing so happy and all even though you ain't got no arms, I changed my mind.' The little bastard looked up at me with tears in his eyes and said, 'I ain't dancing, bitch, my balls itch and I can't scratch them.'"

The joke made Chemah smile. He thought her humor was raw, but other people at the club were rolling in their seats, so he assumed he was simply out of touch.

"I'm serious, you have to be careful of what you tell people. I told this guy I was dating, 'I hear what other people see.' He was cool with that. So later on we're getting busy, I'm all hot and bothered and he asks me, 'Do you want to see me cum, baby, huh? Do you wanna see me cum?' I'm so turned on, I'm like, 'Yeah, baby, I wanna see you cum, I wanna see you cum.' Do you know this motherfucker pulled out and came in my ear? That was some bullshit" (loud laughter).

"Recently I got with this new boyfriend and he has some kids. You know how inquisitive kids can be, the little boy is nine and the little girl is three, so they're always wondering how I do things without sight. Instead of trying to explain to them about the power of the other senses, I try a Mr. Science routine I saw when I was a kid. So I sit the little girl in a chair and I blindfold her. I tell her to open her mouth and I unwrap a Hershey's Kiss and put it in her mouth while the little girl waits. I tell her to chew on it and tell me what it is. After a moment I ask, 'Do you know what it is?' and she answers, 'No.' So I say, 'Let me give you a hint. It's brown and it's something your father gets from me every morning before he goes to work.' Before the little girl could say anything else, her brother starts to scream, 'Spit it out, Crystal, it's a piece of ass.' I swear those kids are learning too much."

The crowd loved her material and clapped loudly when she exited the stage. They had left Base at home, which meant that Chemah had to be her eyes for the night. He rushed to Michelle's side, walking swiftly from the opposite side of the stage and waited for her to find his arm. He had been directed by her earlier not to grab or hold her. "The person who's being led does the holding," she had instructed patiently.

He could tell that she had given the instructions often and was being careful not to patronize him as she told him things that were so obvious you were likely to forget them. "When I stop, you stop," Michelle had said after a few mishaps. He'd felt like a dick and thought to himself that he would give Base a steak when he got home. *This seeing-eye shit is hard,* he thought.

‡‡‡

"How was I? Did I kill 'em or what?" Michelle asked Chemah.

"It was tight, baby. You were pretty good," Chemah said, downplaying his excitement for her.

Michelle knew what he was doing. "Just pretty good, huh? Coming from your tight ass, I'll call that a compliment."

"Baby, I'm not a tight ass. I simply don't like everything you have to say."

"Please, boy, your ass is so tight that if you backed into a wall, you'd suck a brick out of it."

Chemah smiled. Trading quips was their way of showing affection. He opened his mouth to say something else, but thought better of it. She was in rare form tonight and was liable to do a whole other set of jokes based on him.

Chemah started to lead Michelle toward the stage exit door when they were intercepted by Rhonda.

"Hey, people, you're not leaving already, are you?" Rhonda was blocking their path out of the club, and Chemah instinctively looked around for signs of an ambush. Rhonda leaned forward to hug Michelle and Chemah was forced to release his hold on her. The two women hugged and air kissed the sides of each other's faces. There was no real intimacy in the act and Chemah wondered why women bothered with this perfunctory exchange.

"Yeah, girl, we have to go. Boyfriend here promised to take me to dinner before locking me down again."

Being the gentleman that he was, Chemah didn't hesitate to invite Rhonda along. "We're going over to Justin's for a midnight snack; you're perfectly welcome to come along."

Rhonda sucked her teeth in disappointment. "*Tsk*, I have to wait around for the last three sets to be over, but if you don't mind waiting about an hour, I could eat some smothered chicken."

Before Chemah could agree to wait, Michelle nipped the idea in the bud. "I'm sorry, baby," she said in her sweetest voice. "Chemah's babysitter is expecting us by one at the latest and we really have to get going."

Chemah looked puzzled for a moment. He didn't know that Michelle and Ms. Richmond had agreed on a time for them to get home. In the past, whenever he'd had to go out late at night Ms. Richmond had been very accommodating. She'd told Chemah on many occasions that he shouldn't rush back home from his engagement, as the children always slept over at her home and used the beds that her grown children had left behind. The children liked the adventure of sleeping somewhere other than their own beds, and he would always have a fancy breakfast waiting for them when they walked over the next morning. Rhonda gave Chemah a questioning look and Chemah shrugged his shoulders, not knowing what else to say.

"Okay, but we really have to get together soon to discuss your next move. Diddy is still looking for cutting-edge talent for next year's Bad Boys of Comedy. If you hadn't disappeared for the last two months I probably could have still talked him into using you in the season's last show."

Michelle cut her off. "Call me tomorrow and we'll talk about it."

Rhonda turned her face up in disgust and almost snarled. "I don't think so, miss, you are not playing me like that again," she said just as abruptly. The code of conduct that close girlfriends had indicated that each should talk to the other civilly in mixed company, but that code was about to be breached.

"If you think that I'm going to continue to run after your raggedy ass to try and save your career, you're out of your fucking mind. I've been calling you for weeks now and I haven't heard hide nor hair from you. If you don't give a shit about your career anymore, then I can't help you."

Chemah was awestruck. He had been witness to Michelle's fury on more than one occasion in the past couple of months, and he expected her to answer Rhonda in kind at such an affront. Instead, Michelle stood listening to the tirade, looking bored. After a moment she answered.

"Are you finished, heifer?"

Rhonda stood her ground. Her arms were folded over her chest and she waited. "Mmm" was her only response. Michelle turned to the empty space where Chemah was standing a moment before and asked the emptiness, "Chemah, do you think I could have a moment alone with my friend?"

Chemah answered, "Sure" from five feet left of the space Michelle was talking to and Michelle turned again to where his voice came from and said, "Thank you."

Chemah intended to listen to what Michelle was going to say as he walked back to the other side of the stage, but she waited until he was a good distance away before she started talking. From that side, he couldn't hear what the two women were saying, but there sure was a lot of head shaking and hand waving going on between them. Chemah didn't take his eyes off the two women; they looked like two pugilists ready to take a swing at each other. If Michelle weren't blind, they might have been an even match. As it was, he thought Rhonda could take her easily.

After about a minute Rhonda's hands were on her hips and she was nodding in what seemed like agreement with what Michelle was saying. Moments later, Rhonda leaned forward, gave Michelle a warm embrace and a lingering kiss on the cheek. When the two women separated, Rhonda walked away, leaving Michelle standing by herself. Rhonda walked past Chemah as he walked toward Michelle.

"I'll see you next week," Rhonda informed him with a big grin on her face.

Chemah couldn't help himself. He turned and watched the beautiful woman walk away, admiring the way her hips swayed with each step that she took. Rhonda looked over her shoulder at Chemah and caught him admiring her ass. Instead of the approving smile he had received during their lunch date together, what he got was a freakish growl and a nasty soul-piercing look.

Rhonda's response caught Chemah by surprise causing him to trip over his own foot as he made his way back to Michelle.

"Is everything all right between you and Rhonda?" he asked.

"Everything's fine now," Michelle said, reaching out to search for Chemah's arm. She found his arm and looped her own through it. "I had to set her straight on what would be allowed and what wouldn't."

"Such as…?"

"Such as, you two can't decide when or where I can perform without talking to me first."

"Is that all?" Chemah said as he pushed through the exit door leading the way out onto Broadway. "I didn't mean anything by that. I thought you wanted to get back to work as quickly as possible."

"Yeah, that's what I mean. You keep trying to think for me and you can't even think for yourself. Which brings me to the second thing I told her."

"And what was that?" Chemah asked, as he reached into his pocket for his car keys.

"I had to let her know that she was out of place with the game she was running on you."

"Game? What game?" Chemah asked.

"The game she was running on you when she took you to lunch."

Chemah almost dropped his car keys down the grating on the sidewalk as he was enlightened to his own naiveté.

"Not to worry, baby, she's on our side now. She respects that you're mine and she's not going to move on me."

Chemah opened the car door and helped Michelle in without saying anything else. Now he understood the look that Rhonda had given him before they'd left the club. *How dare you look at another woman when your own woman can't look at her man?* Rhonda must have been thinking.

"So now I belong to you?" Chemah asked as he got into the driver's side of the car and reached over to help Michelle with her seat belt.

Michelle's dead eyes seemed to penetrate his own as she turned her head toward the driver's side. "I haven't decided yet, baby, but if you decide you belong to me before I decide, I'll be expecting a few changes in both of our lives. The least of which is you'll have to kiss me at least once."

"I didn't know..." Chemah started to explain before Michelle put her hand up for him to be quiet.

"Now you know, but don't get it twisted, because you aren't getting anywhere tonight anyway. Watching my girl's ass while I'm right there."

"How...?"Chemah stuttered.

"That girl doesn't growl unless someone's sniffing too close. You were the only one that close." Chemah couldn't think of anything else to say, so he started the car. What do you say to a woman who can tell what you're doing without having seen you do it? He was heading toward Justin's restaurant when Michelle said, "I'm not really hungry anymore, let's go home and get the kids."

Chemah was hungry and almost protested, but when he looked over at Michelle and took in the totality of her beauty, he changed his mind. There's nothing that he would deny her. He knew she loved the kids. He hated using his own kids, but if that were the way to her heart, then use them he would. "They're probably still up," he said. "Why don't we pick up some White Castle burgers on the way home?"

Michelle only nodded her consent, but it made him feel good that they finally agreed on something.

Chapter 18

FATHER, DADDY, PATER

A silent and sulking figure had ordered the driver to follow Chemah and Michelle in his yellow cab, from the time they had left the club. Chemah had been driving a mile before he noticed that the same yellow cab was staying five car lengths behind him for some time. Chemah didn't want to alarm Michelle, and continued talking to her as if all was still well, while trying to figure out who was tailing them.

Chemah headed toward Riverside Park, where he knew there would be little to no traffic around when he stopped the car. If the cab stopped behind him, he would jump out and accost the driver.

Chemah pulled over to the curb and opened his car door abruptly. "Are we home already?" Michelle asked.

"No, stay in your seat and don't move or open the doors until I come back," Chemah ordered.

Michelle was startled by what she heard in Chemah's voice and wanted to question him further, but he had already slammed the car door and left her alone.

Chemah had already unholstered his firearm and was walking swiftly toward the cab that had stopped fifteen yards behind him when the back door of the cab opened. Chemah raised his gun and pointed it at the man who was getting out of the backseat.

"Freeze, don't move another fucking muscle," Chemah shouted as he continued to advance upon the cab.

Chemah was surprised to see that it was a short, balding man of approximately sixty years of age who was getting out of the cab. Chemah still took no chances. "Turn around and get your hands up in the air.

The man did as he was ordered as Chemah reached the driver side of the cab. Chemah pointed his gun at the driver and said, "Get out." The driver looked scared out of his wits and stumbled from the car trying to explain that he was only following the orders of his passenger, who had told him to follow the black BMW truck. Chemah believed the driver. The man's turban had been turned askew while he was trying to get out of the car, and he wasn't trying to move to fix it as Chemah pointed the gun away from him and concentrated on the man whose back was to him. Chemah walked right behind the man, who still had his hands up in the air, and reached into the inside of his coat pocket in search of identification. Chemah found the wallet and opened it up to reveal a driver's license with the name Rufus Thomas on it. Chemah immediately recognized it as Michelle's father's name and asked the man to turn around. Chemah handed the man back his wallet and put his firearm back into his shoulder holster. The man glowered at Chemah as he put his wallet back into his pocket.

"Mr. Thomas, I'm Detective Rivers," Chemah said, offering the man his hand to shake.

Michelle's father ignored Chemah's outstretched hand and Chemah retracted it after an uncomfortable amount of time. "I would like to speak to my daughter, if you don't mind," Mr. Thomas announced, more than requested.

"Mr. Thomas, I know you have a lot of questions about what's going on with your daughter—," Chemah said, but before he could complete his sentence, the elder man pushed past him and headed for Chemah's car. Chemah could have easily stopped him, but thought it would not be prudent to put his hands on the man who might one day have to give his consent for Chemah to marry his daughter. Chemah followed closely behind the man as he marched toward the Beemer.

When Mr. Thomas reached the passenger side door, he rapped on the window twice and so hard that Chemah was afraid the glass might shatter. The sound startled Michelle, but her father gave no notice that he was concerned.

"Open the door, Michelle," he said in a tone that said he meant business.

"Daddy, is that you?" Michelle asked, sitting upright and fixing her hair, as if she were a teenager caught making out by a cop or a parent.

"Open this door," Mr. Thomas said again, this time grabbing the handle of the door and pulling hard. Michelle attempted to open the door, but couldn't. Chemah used the remote control door opener to pop the lock before Mr. Thomas could pull on the handle again. The next time he pulled on the handle the door opened so easily that Mr. Thomas was pulled off balance by the force that he used. He righted himself immediately and reached into the truck to pull Michelle out. Michelle felt his grip against her upper arm and yanked herself away from him before he could move her. "What do you think you're doing?" Michelle screamed at him.

Mr. Thomas was not deterred. He reached for her arm again, but this time when he grabbed her, she started swinging her arms wildly, accidentally striking her father in the head.

Michelle's father looked horror stricken that his daughter had struck him.

"Is this what you've come to Michelle, hitting your father and living with some Rastafarian, gun-toting drug dealer?"

"Daddy, stop it," Michelle cried out over her father's ranting.

Chemah was glad they were in a relatively deserted area. All the screaming they were doing would have brought the cops around in any other area. The yellow cab that Michelle's father had gotten out of had left as soon as he and Mr. Thomas had walked away, so he didn't want to get in the Beemer and drive away, leaving the man to fend for himself.

Michelle's scream seemed to have sobered Mr. Thomas, who stared tight-lipped at his daughter, breathing heavily through his nose with his hands on his hips.

"Chemah is not a drug dealer, he is a police detective and I certainly don't live with him."

It took Michelle ten minutes to explain to her father why she was with Chemah and why he was assigned to protect her. She told him how she was attacked in her apartment and about the safe house she was now staying in until her attacker was captured or until the police thought it was safe for her to return home again. She left out the fact that the safe house was in fact Chemah's house, and that she was helping him take care of his kids while he worked at finding the Street Sweeper. Her father asked her why she couldn't stay in her own family's house. There were enough people there to take care of her and protect her at all hours of the day and night.

It was an old argument that she didn't want to get into, so she explained that it was a police decision and they thought it best to put her where no one else knew her.

Mr. Thomas grumbled something about, "Bastards can't find one damn person, and they're going to protect my baby," but didn't elaborate when Chemah shifted from one foot to the other in discomfort.

Michelle changed the subject. "How's Momma, Daddy?"

"She's worried about you, but she's fine. Your brothers and their kids give her enough to stay busy with. She doesn't complain about you not calling, but I know inside it really hurts her how you've stayed away from the family."

"Daddy, I know I've been some trouble, but as soon as this is all over with, I swear I'll come home to visit."

"And when is that going to be?" He looked over at Chemah.

Michelle didn't answer, waiting for Chemah to come to her rescue. Chemah didn't want to give any false hope, but was put on the spot.

"Soon, sir, very soon."

"Yes, that's what I thought," Mr. Thomas said in a condescending manner. He turned back to his daughter. "Promise me you'll give your mother a call first thing tomorrow," he said.

"I promise, Daddy."

"Good. Now give me a big kiss and a hug," he said, reaching into the cab of the truck to hug his daughter for the first time since their last argument. The hug felt good to both of them and they were both sorry to have to let each other go.

When Michelle's father finally let go, he turned to Chemah. "Do you think

I can get a ride to the train station? It appears that I've lost my ride."

"Sure, sir, that'll be no problem at all." Chemah reached for the back door and held it open for the elder man. Michelle's father gave him another dirty look for treating him like an invalid, but jumped into the car without saying anything. Chemah then closed Michelle's door and went around to the driver's side.

Chemah turned the ignition and put the car in gear, but then had a thought.

"Mr. Thomas, if you don't mind me asking, how did you find Michelle?"

"It was easy. She's a comedienne, and eventually she had to work. Every day I checked all the web sites for comedy clubs to see who was working. Last night her name was on the list at Caroline's."

Chemah hadn't thought of that. It was careless of him. If the Street Sweeper knew her profession and had any sense he would do the same thing.

Mr. Thomas read his mind. "That's right, Sherlock, it was that easy to get to you."

Michelle giggled, and whispered to Chemah, "Does he remind you of anyone?"

Chemah knew she was referring to the other day when she had told him, "You're just like my father."

Chemah didn't find that amusing, and thought, *Damn, the whole family's got jokes.*

Chapter 19
MOMMA SAID KNOCK U OUT

It was approximately 12:30 in the afternoon when Chemah got the call from Tatsuya's school. He and Keith Medlin were on their way back to the precinct when his cellphone rang. The woman on the other end spoke softly, but with authority, and Chemah thought he almost recognized the voice.

"Hello, may I speak to Mr. Rivers, please?" the woman's voice said

Chemah felt his stomach turn. Everyone called him Chemah or Detective Rivers. The only time anyone called him Mr. Rivers was when it pertained to his children. A feeling of dread came over him as he answered, "Yes, this is Mr. Rivers," trying to control the anxiety in his voice.

"I'm glad I was able to catch you, Mr. Rivers. I tried your home number, but no one answered. I left a message on your answering machine just in case."

"I'm sorry, who am I speaking to?" Chemah asked.

"Oh my, I'm sorry, this is Mrs. Whales, the school principal at Tatsuya and Héro's school."

Chemah's stomach did a somersault with a half twist. "Yes, Mrs. Whales, is something wrong?" Chemah asked, knowing there could be no other reason for the phone call.

"I'm sorry to say so, but there has been another problem with Tatsuya. He's been in another fight and you know that our school policy is that the parent of anyone fighting in school has to come in no matter who's at fault," the principal explained.

"Yes, I understand, Mrs. Whales. I'm on my way right now. Is Tatsuya all right?" Chemah asked, scared of the answer.

"He seemed to be all right, except for a few scrapes, but I sent him to the school nurse about five minutes ago to be on the safe side. He should be back in my office by the time you get here," Mrs. Whales said, relieving some of Chemah's anxiety.

"Thank you, Mrs. Whales. I'll see you in a few minutes." Chemah breathed a deep sigh and pressed "end" on his cellphone.

"Problems on the home front?" Keith asked.

"Yeah," Chemah said. "You got a problem with me making a stop before we go back in?" he asked his partner.

Keith shrugged. "I'm good for the afternoon. Anything I can help with?"

Chemah shook his head no, not wanting to give up too much information about his family life. "Have to stop by Tatsuya and Héro's school," he said. "Shouldn't take too long."

"Didn't you tell me your little girl Hera was only three years old?" Keith asked. "How is she in the same school as your boy?"

"My girl's name is Héro," Chemah said, correcting the mispronunciation of his daughter's name. "And yes, they do go to the same school. It's a private school and they have a pre-K program. They let the kids in as long as they're potty-trained."

Chemah spoke with a finality that made Keith understand that no more questions about his children would be entertained. "Cool," was all he said. He felt Chemah exert some of the power of the BMW through a snap in his neck as the car lunged forward. Another almost imperceptible nudge of the gas pedal and the car was going in and out of traffic. Keith decided to ease back and take advantage of the comfort that the luxury car allowed him. If Chemah was going to get them killed anyway, he might as well at least enjoy the ride.

Ten minutes later Keith opened his eyes as he felt the car start to slow down. As they were reaching the front of the school, Chemah saw Ms. Richmond and Michelle reach the top of the stairs at the main entrance and allowed the car to coast as he watched them go inside. He hoped Keith wasn't paying attention at that particular moment or he would have a lot of explaining to do. For a moment, Chemah thought he saw recognition in Keith's face as he glanced in the direction of the building entrance, but when Keith didn't say anything, Chemah continued to drive farther up the street. Chemah didn't bother looking for a parking space. He double-parked the car, giving him a reasonable alibi for leaving Keith in the car while he went inside.

"You don't mind waiting in the car a while," Chemah said before Keith had a chance to completely unfasten his seat belt.

"I'm good right here, go handle your business," Keith said.

As Chemah began to climb out of the SUV, Keith's hand reached out and grasped him by the shoulder, stopping him from putting his other foot down on the ground. Chemah looked over his shoulder back at Keith, his expression was one of impatience. "You know this is a no-parking zone, if the cops come and want me to move, I'll need the keys," Keith said, letting go of Chemah's shoulder and extending his hand to accept the keys.

Chemah pursed his lips and then turned his back on Keith, letting the other foot settle on the ground and closing the car door before he bothered to speak.

"Good try, kid, but that's a no go," he said through the open window. "No one drives this car but me. If the cops come you show them your shield, and tell them to keep it moving," Chemah instructed him.

"C'mon, Rivers, I'm not going anywhere, bruh. You could at least let me keep the music on."

Chemah gave him a suspicious look, but then relented. The kid hadn't asked to be dragged along and he had been cool about it thus far. He pushed his hand through the window, extending it and the keys to Keith. Keith smiled enthusiastically and almost snatched the keys out of Chemah's hand. Chemah grimaced as he pulled his hand back through the window. "DO NOT move this car," he said through the window at the smiling, dark-skinned version of himself.

"Yeah, yeah, I heard you," Keith said, waving him off.

Chemah walked back up the block to the front entrance of the school. Before he reached the middle of the steps to the school, he abruptly heard Kanye West bursting out of a car stereo: "JESUS WALKS. JESUS WALKS WITH ME, WITH ME, WITH ME." Chemah knew it was coming from his car and imagined that his woofers were blown and he would need a new amplifier. He gritted his teeth and forced himself not to turn back around. He needed to deal with the Tatsuya situation and he was already angry at the idea of Tatsuya taking another beating. At this point, he felt like giving a beating, and he didn't need his partner to be the one to bear the brunt of his anger. He walked through the school entrance, the echo of Kanye's song following him down the hall.

Chemah walked into the school's main office and saw four boys sitting on the bench that Tatsuya had been sitting on the last time he had been in the school to deal with this same problem. The boys all had an assortment of visible cuts and bruises, including black eyes and busted lips. Chemah didn't see Tatsuya and thought he must have been sent back to class to keep him away from these boys, who had obviously been in a gang fight.

The school secretary noticed him standing in the doorway and jumped to her feet immediately. "They're waiting for you in the principal's office," she said, escorting him to the wooden door to her left. It didn't dawn on Chemah that neither Michelle nor Ms. Richmond were anywhere to be seen until he neared the door, whose doorknob the secretary was now turning. Before the door was fully open, Chemah heard the angry and accusatory voices of men and women.

As he crossed the threshold to the door, the angry voices stopped and two men and four of the five women in the room turned to stare at him. The exception was Michelle, who didn't need to see him to know he was there. The principal, Mrs. Whales, came from behind her desk to greet Chemah.

"It's good to see you, Mr. Rivers." she said, seeming more relieved than glad to see him.

"Where's Tatsuya?" Chemah said, calmly addressing his first concern.

"He's right there." The principal pointed behind Chemah and to the right.

Tatsuya was sitting quietly with his hands folded in his lap. When Chemah turned to look at him, the boy's face was unwavering. Chemah gazed deeply into the boy's eyes from where he stood, looking for fear or shame, and found none. Chemah walked over to his son and bent down on one knee to check him more closely.

"Are you okay?" Chemah asked, holding the boy's chin as he turned his curly head from left to right, looking for bruises. Tatsuya nodded his head yes, and then the room exploded in a commotion again.

"Is he all right? Of course he's all right. That little animal should be behind bars," Chemah heard a woman's voice say.

Before Chemah could turn back toward the small group of adults again, he heard Michelle intercede. "Animal? Who the hell are you calling an animal? Your kid is one of that pack of fucking hyenas that go around the school looking for smaller children to prey on," she said in the direction of the woman who'd accused Tatsuya. "Well, this time they bit off more than they could chew."

Before Michelle could say anything else, the principal stepped into the middle of the group and spoke up. "I understand this is very upsetting for everyone, but please refrain from name calling and vulgar language," she said. "That kind of language is totally unnecessary in a place where we're trying to set an example for children."

"An example for children!" Michelle looked like she was going out of her mind. "Is that what you call it when you continue to allow bullies to attack younger, unsuspecting students? All the money that we pay for our children to be educated here and all you can say is 'no name calling'? This whole damn school is a fucking farce. I'm glad Tatsuya whipped all their asses," she yelled.

Chemah came to attention at this time. He now understood what had transpired.

"Low-class savage," the woman closest to Chemah whispered.

Chemah frowned, but was in no mood to chastise anyone for being rude.

"What the fuck did you say, bitch? I know you didn't call me a savage," Michelle turned and screamed in the direction of the woman.

Not meaning for anyone to have heard her comment, the woman was startled and looked around as if Michelle couldn't possibly have been talking to her. When the woman didn't respond right away, Michelle continued, "Say that shit again, bitch. I dare you to say that shit again."

Now it appeared as if Michelle was looking directly at the woman. Ms. Richmond grabbed Michelle by the top part of her arm as if she were about to guide her away, but Michelle shook her off and lunged at the woman who had insulted her.

Chemah was in front of the woman before Michelle got to her. Chemah caught Michelle by her two raised fists and put her arms to her sides as he started to lead her to the door, with Ms. Richmond following close behind. This did not deter Michelle who continued to struggle and shout obscenities.

"I'll be back for you, bitch," she called over Chemah's shoulder. "You're lucky I'm blind, I would've checked your jaw a long time ago if I still had my sight. And all the rest of you motherfuckers better watch your back," Michelle continued, addressing the small retinue of shocked parents. "If I ever have to come back here for anything more than a fucking awards ceremony, I will burn this goddamn school to the ground."

Chemah got Michelle out of the door and almost slammed the door on Ms. Richmond as she came out of the door with Tatsuya in tow.

When the door closed Chemah felt Michelle relax in his arms. She blew out her breath in an exaggerated exhalation.

"Whew, that was fun," she said into Chemah's ear.

"What, you were faking all that?" Chemah said in a low tone between his clenched teeth.

"Good cop-bad cop, baby," she spoke into his ear again. "Go do your thing. If you don't fix this, they're going to throw the kid out of the school. He beat up six boys. One of them had to go to the hospital with his parents." Michelle now sounded concerned.

"And you thought making a scene in there is going to help the situation?" Chemah said, still talking to her through clenched teeth.

"Better that they're thinking about what a crazy, blind lady is going to do than what a scared boy already did," Michelle said in a matter-of-fact manner.

Chemah was exasperated. He knew Michelle had good intentions, but was not used to following anyone else's lead. Chemah was glad Michelle couldn't see the feeling of adoration in his eyes.

"I'll fix it," he said, nudging Michelle toward Ms. Richmond.

Ms. Richmond took Michelle by the elbow and Michelle finally allowed herself to be held. Ms. Richmond gave Chemah a reasonably filthy look, as if he had done something wrong to her. He shrugged his shoulders up at her, as if to say, "What did I do?" Ms. Richmond set her mouth like his mother used to when she was finished with him, and then said, "Go on."

Chemah walked back into the principal's office for the second time and every one of the parents turned to him with scared, questioning eyes. He'd seen that look before in perps that he and his partners had worked. Michelle had been right in playing the good cop-bad cop game. When perps looked as scared as these people looked, they were usually ready to cut a deal. "She's starting to calm down now," Chemah started.

"Exactly who was that, Mr. Rivers?" asked Principal Whales.

Chemah smiled his most disarming smile. "I'm sorry, that was my fiancée. She's very protective of the children, but don't worry, I'm not going to sue anyone, no matter what she says."

"You're thinking of suing the school?" Principal Whales seemed more afraid than the parents.

"Well, she was really talking about suing the parents of the boys who jumped Tatsuya," Chemah said, pointing at the huddled parents. Chemah noticed they all blanched at his words. "But I wouldn't sue the school, either. As long as Tatsuya's physically and emotionally well, I won't ever consider suing the school."

"The school nurse says she couldn't find anything wrong with him, but a few scratches on his knuckles," Principal Whales exclaimed.

"Physically he seems fine, Principal Whales, but we don't know what kind of post-traumatic stress his little mind is going through with this whole ordeal. I think the best thing to do is to keep the young men that jumped Tatsuya home for a few days, to make sure that everyone involved realizes the seriousness of their actions."

Before any of the parents could open their mouths to object, Chemah continued, "I don't think they warrant any more punishment than that. My partner out in the car tried to convince me that we could get a couple of juvie assault collars out of this," Chemah said, chuckling for effect. "But I don't need the extra paperwork right now and, to tell you the truth, I wouldn't feel right doing that to all of your families. No, I think the boys have learned enough of a lesson. Ms. Whales, my fiancée and the babysitter will be taking both of the children out of the school for the rest of the day. If you could arrange for someone to bring Héro down from her class, they'll be waiting for her in your outer office. I can't stay and wait for her to come down, but could you give me another minute in your outer office with my fiancée before you come out? I want to assure her that everything has been properly handled so that she won't go berserk again."

"Of course, Mr. Rivers, take as much time as you need," the principal answered.

Chemah didn't give any of the other parents an opportunity to say anything. He turned on his heels and walked out of the door.

‡‡‡

Michelle heard the doorknob turn before the door opened and was already facing the door when Chemah came out. She was concerned that Chemah was back out of the room so soon. Ms. Richmond saw Chemah and stood closer to Michelle, as if protecting her.

"They're sending for Héro," Chemah said as he stood in front of the two women. "I've convinced them that it would be wise for everyone that the boys that jumped Tatsuya be kept home for a few days."

Michelle smiled at this information, but Ms. Richmond stayed tight lipped.

"I have to get back to work. Ms. Richmond, if you could make sure they all get back to my house safely, I would appreciate it." The older woman nodded her agreement. "They'll be coming out of the office any minute now, try not to attack anyone," Chemah said to Michelle with a smile in his voice.

Michelle recognized it and smiled back up at him. Chemah couldn't help himself, he leaned over and kissed Michelle on the nose. "Thank you," he said to her tenderly.

"Aaahh, it was nothing," she said, playing it off.

Ms. Richmond, who had not left Michelle's side, sniffed up at Chemah. She didn't say anything, but Chemah could tell that she was pleased.

"I'm going to talk to Tatsuya for a second and then I have to get back to work," he said. Michelle nodded okay and Chemah walked the two steps to where Tatsuya was sitting on the bench outside of the principal's office.

The principal's secretary had the presence of mind to send the assaultive boys back to their classes before Chemah had come out of the office. Kneeling down to talk to his son at this bench was like déjà vu for Chemah, it seemed like he had done it too often.

"You want to tell me what happened," Chemah asked his son.

Tatsuya shrugged and began to talk. "They were picking on Héro," Tatsuya said, looking at the floor to avoid his father's eyes. When his father didn't respond, the boy looked up from the floor. "I didn't want to do it, Dad," the boy said in earnest. "I told them to leave her alone, but they wouldn't listen. And I kept remembering what Michelle always says," Tatsuya continued.

"What does Michelle always say?" Chemah asked Tatsuya and glanced quickly over to Michelle, who was listening intently to the conversation.

"She said always take care of your family, they're all you have," the boy quoted.

Chemah looked over his shoulder at Michelle again and smiled his appreciation to her, willing his emotions into her from where he kneeled. Michelle was smiling so broadly that Chemah thought his sentiments were reaching her.

"And she also told me," Tatsuya continued, "that if anybody ever bothers my sister, I should…" Tatsuya's voice trailed off.

"Should what?" Chemah asked.

Tatsuya looked to Michelle and then back to Chemah, then said, "She said I should put foot to ass and knock those motherf'ers out," Tatsuya said guiltily.

Chemah looked over to Michelle again, but now she wasn't smiling anymore. She looked quite guilty and did her best Stevie Wonder impression, her head swaying from side to side in imitation of other blind people she remembered from when she could see.

"Don't worry, son, you did the right thing," Chemah said, taking his son into his arms and hugging him. Chemah held his son briefly, then held him away from himself. "Tatsuya, I want you to go home with your sister, Michelle, and Ms. Richmond. I have to go back to work. As far as I'm concerned there's nothing more to talk about, but if you ever feel like you have to defend yourself or your sister again, you have my permission to…" Chemah looked over at Michelle again, "'put foot to ass' if you have to."

Chemah walked out of the school and toward his car, a smile on his face the whole way. The music was still blaring out of his car speakers, but he didn't give it a second thought. He opened the driver side door and hopped into the seat, making the car bounce with his weight.

"Everything all right?" Keith asked him over the loud music.

"Everything is fine," Chemah answered, turning the key that was already in the ignition. Chemah was in such a good mood he didn't bother to lower the volume on the hip-hop music that was kicking through his system. Chemah eased away from the curb, and later would vehemently deny to Keith that earlier that day he was nodding his head to Fifty Cent's latest release. He liked Fifty's music. As of late, he hated agreeing with Keith.

Chapter 20
PICKING UP THE PIECES

Kat opened the door of the Bentley for herself, and held the door open, waiting for Margarita to step out into the afternoon sunshine. Margarita took her time getting out of the car, as always, trying to make her entrance or appearance anywhere she went as dramatic as possible. The last time Margarita had been to Tavern on the Green was four years ago. Now, two days after being released from jail, she was meeting with her lawyer and her ex-partners in the very private back room of the restaurant.

She'd almost felt insulted when her one-time partners suggested that she not come to meet with them in their Fifth Avenue offices. She'd sold all of her rights to the consultancy firm before she went away to prison and had been paid the millions that her share was worth. She had given Chemah the house and paid him child support and was still a wealthy woman. Wealth, however, did not move her; it was power that had always motivated her life.

They were no more than twenty minutes into the meeting when the two partners who were representing the firm got up from their seats and filed out of the restaurant. Margarita was fuming: *Who the fuck do they think they are? I helped make that firm what it is today. They should be happy to have me back in their midst. I haven't even asked to be reinstated as a partner.*

The truth of the matter was that Margarita had tried to blackmail her way back into the firm under the guise of "helping them with their local partisan remuneration distribution" problem. It was a nice way of saying she knew who, what, where, when, and why they were giving money to certain individuals in the city in order to get their clients elected.

Margarita's lawyer tried to console her by saying that he would contact the partners again and propose a new meeting based on more equitable terms, but in the end Margarita knew that the partners would rather take their chances with the damage that her leaking a negative story about them would cause, rather than lose their whole clientele. It had been a shot in the dark, but ultimately Margarita knew if had she been placed in the same position, she would have vetoed being a partner with an ex-con.

Kat got up from her seat in the corner of the room, sure that she had witnessed her best friend's karma continuing its progression toward her ultimate demise. She wasn't one for doom-and-gloom predictions, but she firmly believed that "what comes around goes around." She knew that Margarita was in for some harder times now that she was back in society. All of the things that were important to her were becoming inaccessible. She had been by Margarita's side this morning when she was talking to Chemah on the phone. Through all of the false bravado she displayed in front of others, Kat could feel the desperation in Margarita's soul. She was hurt to the core when Chemah told her that she would not be able to come to his home to visit her daughter. This was her homegirl. They went way back, like reclining chairs, but what did she expect. After all, she did kill his son's mother. The woman had done some heinous things in her life and Kat wanted to help her pick up the pieces when karma came to get its due.

‡‡‡

Margarita had been there for her during a time when her life was a mess. First helping her with a place to stay when she found herself in an abusive relationship, then helping her pay to finish her degree, and finally getting her a job at the consultancy firm. It had been her decision to move on with Margarita, when the job of commissioner of Community Affairs was offered. Margarita had made her deputy commissioner and although she lost her job when

Margarita went to jail, she had learned enough and eventually borrowed money from Margarita to go into business with an old associate to start an elite car service company. In some ways she felt she owed all of her success to Margarita.

Kat was sure that she was the only person who Margarita had confided in about what had transpired in her life while she was in the penitentiary. It wasn't the kind of thing you talked about openly unless there was a book or movie deal to go with it. This meeting had been another humiliation that she was sure would not be shared with anyone else. "Let's get the hell out of here, girl," Kat said, rubbing the top of her friend's head.

Margarita didn't move. She held her own head in her hands and stifled a moan. Abruptly Margarita looked up at Kat and asked, "How long do we have the car for?"

"For as long as you need, girl. Your money paid for it. You're a partner as far as I'm concerned."

"Thanks, baby, but I don't want to own a car service. Just the use of that beautiful Bentley until I can renew my license and get myself a new Jag."

"The car is no problem, baby, it's not going to turn into a pumpkin after twelve. Where do you want to go from here?" Kat asked Margarita.

Margarita's reply was plain. "I'm going to go see my daughter."

Kat wanted to talk Margarita out of her decision, but knew that it would be a futile gesture. At that moment, she decided that she would no longer follow her good friend. She was leading a good life now and she could not let down the other people that she was responsible for. She had been so preoccupied with getting Margarita situated that she had yet to tell her the good news. She was having a baby. And with that on her mind, the most she could do would be to postpone the inevitable for as long as possible.

"Why don't we go get your hair done first, then we can talk about what you should do next?"

Margarita got up from the table, leaving her lawyer all by himself.

The two women walked toward the door arm in arm. Margarita turned back to the lawyer. "John, stay close to a phone. You may have to bail me out later." Her lawyer opened his mouth to protest, when he saw Kat shaking her head, indicating to him that an argument at this time would not be in his best interest. Instead he nodded his head yes in resignation and reached for the bell that would call the waitress to the table. He was going to need a drink.

Chapter 22

THE BELLY OF THE BEAST

other and son ate breakfast in silence. Victor picked up a crispy piece of bacon and used it to break the yolk of a fried egg. He dunked the bacon in the warm, yellow liquid and shoved it into his mouth without looking up from his plate. He hadn't been to church or to the store in two days, and had no intention of leaving the house anytime soon. He didn't remember how he had gotten home from the party Friday night. His mother had awakened him from a restless sleep the next morning, as if nothing at all had occurred. Now it was Monday morning and she had insisted that he leave the sanctity of his bedroom and eat some home-cooked food. Victor knew she wouldn't leave for the store until he had finished everything on his plate. The sight of her wearing the same house dress that she had worn on Friday was disconcerting to him. The reminder made him swallow the food down quickly as he felt bile rising from his stomach.

‡‡‡

Victor had always been able to walk proudly in his neighborhood without fear of verbal or physical attack since he was a little boy. Now he was afraid to leave the house because he was unsure of how many people knew about what happened at the party. He calculated that the whole neighborhood now knew what kind of loose woman his mother was.

"Are you going to school today?" she asked him between a sip of coffee and a bite of toast. Victor shook his head no, and immediately regretted his answer. His mother immediately got up from her seat and came over to the side of the table where he was sitting. She stood behind him and put her hand to his forehead.

"Are you feeling sick, honey?" she asked, pressing her breasts into the back of his head.

His mouth was full of food, making it hard for him to talk, but he opted to say "no" verbally instead of shaking his head, so that his head didn't unnecessarily move against her breasts.

"What is it then, baby? Why aren't you going out?" she asked, reaching over his shoulder to pick up the plate he had wiped clean with his last piece of toast and moved toward the sink.

Victor was almost moved to tears. He could barely contain his anger. Here he was, on the verge of finishing his penance to God, and his mother had condemned him to a life of shame. Victor pushed himself away from the table with such force that he almost fell backward in his chair. He flailed his arms like a tightrope walker in an attempt to regain his balance. Before he could fully right himself, his mother launched herself from the sink and grabbed him by the upper arm. Her powerful arms, with the strength that stems from the heart of a mother, allowed him to steady himself. It was the same strength that had ripped the sheets while she went through the pain of birthing him into the world. And it seemed, to Victor, at that moment, that she was abnormally strong. As he stood up straight to face his mother, his fists balled up in frustration, his mother looked him up and down and smiled an amused smile. "Well, speak up, boy. If you have something on your mind, come out with it."

Victor's resolve dissolved like Alka Seltzer in warm water when his mother crossed her arms, waiting for his words. Taking the routinely cowardice way out, he lowered his eyes to the floor and turned to go back to his room. Victor was surprised by another show of strength from his mother as she yanked him backward and off his feet by the scruff of his neck and held him up straight in front of her, again preventing him from falling. This time he scowled at her as he shook her hands off of him.

"Boy, I don't care how grown you get, don't you ever turn your back on me when I'm talking to you, do you understand me?"

Victor didn't say anything. He glared back at her, humiliated at how she had manhandled him.

"Now if there is some problem that you have," she continued, "we can talk about it, or if there's something that you can't talk to me about, maybe you can talk to Pastor Fredricks. But there's one thing you can't do and that's stay in the house your whole life. Now you know I don't like you going out all hours of the night like you've been doing as of late, but shuttin' yourself out from the rest of the world is no way to live, either."

Victor could not believe that she had suggested that he talk to the pastor about his problem. If the pastor had not heard about what his mother had done already, he surely would not be the one to out her as a whore. "You think I would have the nerve to tell Pastor what you did Friday night?"

Reesey seemed puzzled. "What I did Friday night? Boy, what are you talking about? So I had a couple of drinks and went to bed. Ain't nobody going to care about that. We're all entitled to let off some steam once in a while. Now, that Miss Watkins, when she drinks, well, she tends to let her mouth carry on too much of her business—"

Victor cut off his mother's inane chattering. "You didn't just have a few drinks, you were drunk. And you didn't simply go to bed, you..." Victor couldn't bring himself to say it. He looked into his mother's eyes and had a clearer understanding of why she was so cavalier. The look on Reesey's face told him she really didn't remember what had transpired last Friday.

"What did I do?" his mother insisted.

Victor looked at her a bit more softly now and said, "Uh, you came out of your room without your robe."

Victor's mother chuckled and patted her son on his shoulder. "Boy, you are a mess. You're more of a prude than some of the old hens in the church choir."

Victor tried to smile at his mother, but it came out as a grimace. Victor's mother studied him for a second and then spoke with a heavy heart.

"Son, if something is really bothering you, you can't keep it bottled up. It'll eat you up inside like a cancer and then what will I do all by myself?" She stroked his face once softly, like she used to when he was a little boy, and then put her coat on and left for the store.

Victor was staring at the door his mother had exited and pondered how he would continue his God-given mission, when an ominous knock came from the door on which he was fixated. The knock woke him from his trance and he walked the few steps to look through the peephole. On the other side of the glass eye stood his childhood friend, Franklyn. Victor was startled to see him on the other side of the door and would probably not have opened it if he'd had the sense to use some stealth when he looked through the peephole. Victor turned the knob of the door slowly and then yanked the door open the way one might rip off a Band-Aid that had been left on too long. Victor looked blankly at Franklyn and Franklyn looked back at Victor, waiting for an invite into the apartment. When none came, Franklyn asked, "Can I come in, dog?"

Victor nodded his head yes and opened the door farther to allow Franklyn in.

"I didn't mean to intrude on you or anything, brother, I have to go back to Boston tomorrow and I thought I'd come check on how you were doing. You weren't doing all that well when we dropped you home Friday night."

Victor hung his head, but appreciated the tactful way that Franklyn had understated the condition he had been in three days ago. "The boys thought I should be the one to come over and tell you that all that shit that happened on the roof will never be spoken about in public again."

Victor looked up into Franklyn's eyes for some sign that he was mocking him and found none. Franklyn guessed Victor's next question and answered it before it was asked.

"Those dudes we met up there on Friday are from Brooklyn. One of them has a cousin on the block who told them about the party. They don't know you or your mother. We ran them all the way back to the A train, after lumping them up a little more," he said with a smirk. "Light-skinned dude was still talking shit when my brother threw his ass over the turnstile." Franklyn felt uncomfortable standing there with Victor not saying anything, so he turned to go. "Like I said, the boys thought you should know. If you ever need anything, man, you can reach out. On the strength of your brother and all, they want you to know you'll always be down with the Fab Five."

Franklyn held his hand out to Victor and Victor took it greedily. He hadn't realized how much he needed a good friend until this moment.

The old friends pulled in one to the other and patted each other on the back for a moment, each one feeling the old camaraderie of their youth fleetingly return until they let each other go. The discomfort that was created by the knowledge that they shared returned immediately when they released their grip and looked into each other's eyes. It was clear that too much had occurred in each of their lives for them to recapture the old friendship. Victor looked at his old friend's back as he walked out the door and almost asked him to stay. He was lonely and needed a friend. He thought that maybe Franklyn would understand what he was trying to do, but when Franklyn reached the stairs and turned to wave one last time, he couldn't bring himself to ask for help.

Moments later, he was alone in the apartment getting dressed to go to school. He almost stopped getting dressed when he realized that tonight might be the night that all his work bore fruit. The anxiety he felt made him nauseated and he swallowed down some bile. The detective who had interrogated him was the only thing that could get in his way. This cop didn't fit in to the plans that he had, but if he got in his way again, he would have no compulsion to spare him. It would be for the greater good.

Chapter 23

Violence Begets Violence

The last day of November was yesterday and with it went the light jackets and sweaters. Today Chemah had to break out the kid's winter coats. He'd had to put one of Tatsuya's old coats on Héro. He hadn't noticed how much she'd grown in one year. After trying on the two coats that she'd worn the previous year and finding that the sleeves on both coats rode high on her forearms, he opted to go into the basement and look for the box that held Tatsuya's old clothes. The box was easy to find, as it was always hard to throw away or give away anything that was a part of his past. Like fond memories of his children in the back of his mind, he stored old and less-used items carefully in the huge sub-basement of the brownstone. There was plenty of room, as the sub-basement was not used for anything else.

Héro was happy when she found out she would be wearing one of her brother's old coats. Chemah rolled up the sleeves so that the jacket fit snuggly at the wrists. The part that draped over her torso fit like a tent. When he was done, Héro ran to show her brother what a big girl she was and how well his coat fit her. Chemah didn't have the heart to tell her that she looked like a poster girl for the Salvation Army hurricane relief program. He'd have to take her to get a new jacket today before they went to the movie that he promised he'd take them to.

Michelle wanted to go with them, but after last night's great show, she knew she should not lose her momentum. Just as she was thinking about how she should be honing her craft, the phone rang. The phone rang three times before

Chemah answered it. By that time Michelle was finished pouring herself a glass of orange juice and was listening to his brief conversation. It was Rhonda on the phone and it upset Michelle when she realized that Rhonda was attempting to have a conversation with Chemah to discuss the possibility of her doing another gig tonight.

Essentially, Rhonda needed another comedian to stand in for the next few nights for a veteran comedian who had gotten sick and had to pull out of the showcase she was producing at the Laff Factory. Chemah walked toward the kitchen with the hands-free phone as he was talking to Rhonda and was smart enough to hand the phone off to Michelle right away without discussing if, when, or where Michelle would do the show. Michelle discussed the details of the gig loud enough for Chemah, who stood next to her in the kitchen, to hear.

"The Laff Factory tonight at ten o'clock, um-hmm. Don't worry, baby, I'm sure you'll find a way to pay me back. ...No, sugar, I mean besides the three hundred dollars for doing the spot tonight. ...No, I'm not doing it for less than that. You know what I usually charge. Only 'cause you're a friend baby, only 'cause you're a friend."

Chemah could only hear Michelle's side of the conversation, but he knew exactly what they were discussing. When Michelle got off the phone, she asked him if he would be able to escort her to another job tonight. Chemah didn't know where this club was and knew he would have no time to reconnoiter the place before they got there. He also knew that if he told her no, she would get up and go on her own, even if it meant taking Base along with her.

"I'm not sure it's such a great idea going to this club without checking it out first," Chemah said. Michelle took a deep breath in preparation to do battle, but before she could get a word in edgewise, Chemah conceded.

"I'm not saying I won't take you, because I know you have to get back to your real life. Just remember that we still do things my way the whole time that we're there."

Michelle could have let Chemah have this small say in the matter, but the show she had done last night had amped her. Now her sense of independence was almost back to what it had been before the whole debacle with the Street Sweeper had begun.

"Why do you always have to try to tell me what I can and can't do?" she asked. "You are not my father, so I don't see why you insist on trying to control every aspect of my life. If you can't respect my opinions, then you can just..."

Chemah didn't want to argue and could see no other way to quiet Michelle, so he did what any other man might have done. He reached over and pulled her to his chest. Michelle's breath left her lungs in a gasp and Chemah pressed his mouth to hers before she could object.

Only Michelle would not object. On the contrary, she had been waiting for a month for Chemah to demand this kiss from her. She didn't wait for his tongue to come sliding sneakily into her mouth; instead, she thrust her own tongue between his lips and urged his tongue to come to life in a dance with her own. Chemah felt his mouth crush against Michelle's. The kiss they were sharing was so violent that he tasted blood in his mouth. He didn't know if it was his or hers and seconds later didn't care who it belonged to. The adrenaline in the blood he had tasted sped through his body, causing him to feel lightheaded and powerful at the same time. Michelle let her splayed fingers roam across the expanse of Chemah's broad back and she could feel his lats flex as if he were about to plunge his dick into her right through her clothes. Before he could do it, she clung to him and jammed her pelvis against his in hope that she would feel his penis begin to stiffen against her.

She loved to feel the beginning of an erection and knew that her vagina would become moist and swollen as she felt his penis lengthen and stiffen just for her. Only this time she was too late to feel Chemah's dick grow hard for her, because as she thrust her hips forward, she stabbed herself in the pubis with the solid mass that was blunted by Chemah's loose-fitting Sean John jeans. Michelle and Chemah looked more like they were wrestling then kissing. One was grabbing the other's hair, while the other was squeezing and kneading the other's buttocks. Their hands were moving all over each other's bodies frantically, as if this were the last time they would ever touch each other again.

The couple continued their ardent groping for what seemed like an eternity to each of them before Michelle could no longer stand the intensity. She grabbed Chemah's hips and forced them away from her through sheer force of will. Chemah broke off their kiss, believing that Michelle had had her fill of the groping that was reminiscent of his teenage years. As her hands reached for and undid his belt in an instant, he knew that his assumption was correct, but what he hadn't counted on was that she would want their passion to escalate right here in the kitchen.

Chemah grabbed Michelle's hands as they were undoing the button on his jeans. "Not now," he whispered to her in a throaty voice that was subdued by the passion that filled his chest.

Michelle did not answer him and her blank eyes, although wide with intensity, showed no sign that she had heard him. She tore her hands from his and clawed at the button at the top of his pants.

As the button popped loose, Chemah grabbed Michelle's hands again and spoke in a more controlled voice. "We can't, the kids are right upstairs."

Michelle snatched her hands from his again and grabbed hold of the front of his pants, ripping the two sides apart so that his zipper was undone.

"I said no," Chemah said through gritted teeth. Before he could reach down to rezip his pants, though, Michelle had her hands on his already hard penis. Michelle made a mental note that Chemah wore no underwear. For the first time in a long time she acknowledged to herself that she missed her sight. She knew in the way that only a woman knows that the sight of this man's open pants with no underwear on would have been a turn-on for any woman. But the thought, even without the sight, had been enough to start her pussy salivating.

Chemah was openly struggling to get Michelle's hands off his penis. If the boys at the precinct could see him now they would laugh him right out of the department. The more he fought, the tighter Michelle would hold on. His struggling only helped Michelle jerk his dick back and forth with more force, which facilitated more blood into his penis, thereby making his penis even harder. After a moment, Chemah stopped struggling. He let his hands fall to the side and gave Michelle full access to what she appeared to want more than anything else. Michelle continued to stroke his penis back and forth for a while before she realized that Chemah had stopped struggling. She stopped jerking his dick for a moment, but continued to hold his blood-filled penis with two hands.

"What's wrong?" she asked, flinging her head up as if she were attempting to stare into his eyes.

"Nothing's wrong, if you don't think that when a person tells you to stop it's still okay to keep going."

"I thought you were trying to keep yourself from coming too fast, I didn't think you were serious," Michelle confessed.

"Well, I am serious, as serious as I'll ever be," Chemah said with conviction. "I told you the kids are right upstairs, they can come down at any moment."

Michelle let go of Chemah's penis as if it were a snake she had been fighting with. "I'm sorry,.I thought it was what we both wanted," she said wearily.

Chemah tried to put his penis back into his pants, but it was so big and hard that it wouldn't fit. After a halfhearted attempt to put it back in, he decided to wait a few moments and let it get softer before trying again.

Michelle was listening for the sound of his zipper going up, but the sound never reached her ears. Leaning back against the kitchen countertop, a thought came to Michelle's mind. Maybe she was being too aggressive. Maybe Chemah needed to feel like he was the one controlling the situation. With that thought in mind, she tried another line of seduction. Unbeknownst to Michelle, Chemah watched her carefully as she started to slowly lift her skirt. She didn't know for sure if Chemah was watching, so she chuckled softly to catch his attention. Chemah didn't know why the chuckle disturbed him, but it did.

As Michelle's skirt reached her midthigh, she began to tease Chemah. "I know what it is, Chemah, you're afraid of my little pussy, aren't you?" Michelle chuckled again for emphasis and raised her skirt all the way past her pantyline, up to her waist. She had taken to buying only pink panties many years ago because her first boyfriend had found them to be so sexy and now only bought them out of habit. Nonetheless she knew that most men found them irresistible. The length of her skirt was bunched in her fist and she opened her legs slowly to show the tiny pink panties that she knew would keep Chemah's dick hard.

Chemah couldn't stop looking between Michelle's legs. The panties barely covered her pubic mound and he could see a spreading wet stain in the middle of the patch of cloth that covered the thick pussy lips that he knew were hidden behind the sheer cloth.

Michelle could hear Chemah's breath coming in short and shallow wisps. She needed to do something to take him over the edge, and she remembered the day he had watched her masturbate from the safety of the upstairs hallway. With her free hand she pulled the flimsy panties to the side exposing her swollen genitalia. "Isn't it still pretty, Chemah? Or is all you ever want to do is merely look at it?" As Chemah stared openly at Michelle's private parts, the lips that were stuck together by her copiously secreting vagina started to slowly part. To Chemah, they were a beacon beckoning him to enter into a safe haven.

Michelle had always kept her vagina tight by practicing her Kegel exercises. Now with her labia swollen open to the point that you could easily see inside her, when she flexed the muscles inside her vagina it gave the appearance of a sucking mouth. The sight was more than Chemah could stand.

The two steps closing the gap between him and Michelle were bridged instantaneously. Chemah reached between Michelle's legs and relieved Michelle of the sheer material she was holding aside to expose herself. With a quick tug of his hand, he tore the panties away from Michelle's body. Michelle felt the quick pain of the broken elastic as it snapped against her waist and winced, then pouted in an attempt to play the submissive.

At this point, Chemah no longer cared what she was playing at. He got between her legs and bent low at the waist. Before Michelle knew what was going on, he had an arm hooked under each leg and then lifted her off the ground with what seemed like ease to her. Michelle instinctively wrapped her arms around his neck to prevent herself from falling backward. As she attempted to interlace her fingers behind his neck for security, Michelle felt Chemah move toward her womb in one powerful and sensuous thrust, sending shockwaves to her eardrums that made them feel like they had exploded from the force that his penis had manifested.

Now that Chemah was firmly lodged in her, he felt no need to rush to completion. Chemah allowed his hips to leisurely slide backward as he held Michelle's body steady in his arms. He felt her vulva drag raggedly against his penis as he pulled away, grudgingly clinging to his shaft and leaving a trail of vaginal juices in its wake. Chemah slammed into her again, but this time Michelle was braced for the impact. Her eyelids closed over her blank eyes as she surrendered herself to the pleasure that only Chemah's body could now give her. Her head lolled back and she opened her soul to him so that she would be able to enjoy the pleasure that his hard cock afforded her, tilting her hips up to yield to him.

Chemah had been so lost in the void of his own purgatory these past two years that he had deprived himself of the comforts of a woman. Now he let himself get lost in the throes of his own damnable passion. That's why he didn't hear his children clamoring down the stairs.

When Michelle heard them, her eyelids snapped open like broken shutters. They were still two floors up, but they would be at the bottom of the stairs in a minute and soon after they would head for the kitchen. She was sorry it had to end, but there was no way she was going to allow those children to see her and their father getting freaky on the kitchen counter.

"Chemah, stop, the kids are coming," Michelle implored him. "Chemah, the kids are coming," she repeated, this time more earnestly.

Chemah was so lost in his own desires that he could not hear Michelle's words.

Michelle could hear the children begin their descent down the stairs and quickly made the decision to do the only thing that would ensure that a man would stop fucking. She had to make him cum. Michelle began to work her hips faster against his. She whispered fiercely into his ear, "Cum for me, baby. Come on. You can do it. Faster, faster, honey. Come on, you can do it, cum for

Michelle, cum for me, baby, hurry, cum for me."

Michelle could hear the children on the second landing now and became desperate in her pleas to Chemah. "Hurry, baby, hurry. I can't stand it anymore, I need to feel you wet me inside, hurry." In her desperation, Michelle attempted to shake Chemah out of his trance, shaking him by the neck that she was already precariously clinging to. "Chemah, let go, you have to let it go, baby, come on, baby, cum for Michelle."

When Michelle heard the children reach the bottom of the stairs, she threw all caution to the wind. She released the grip she had on Chemah's neck with her left hand and leaned back for leverage as Chemah continued to assault her vagina. "Cum, motherfucker," she said as she slapped Chemah in the face with all her strength.

When the blow struck his face, Chemah thrust upward one last time and Michelle felt his hot seed splash her inside. Chemah spasmed five times before he opened his eyes, and then he heard his children in the living room right outside of the kitchen door. He almost dropped Michelle on the floor when he realized that his pants were around his ankles and his children were only a couple of yards away. In a moment of clarity he put her down gently on the counter and started to quickly pull himself together.

"Daddy, we're ready," Héro shouted from the living room.

Michelle hopped down from the kitchen counter and easily fixed her skirt before making her way along the counter and toward the kitchen door. Chemah was still trying to fix himself up. Although he had been able to fit his penis back into his pants, it was still semi-erect and he preferred to give it more time to return to normal before he went out to the living room to greet his kids. He looked down at the floor and spotted the remains of Michelle's underwear. He picked them up and almost threw them in the garbage, but decided against it and instead thrust them deep into his back pocket to be discarded later. He didn't know what had come over him. It was as if he couldn't control himself when he saw Michelle's pussy.

Moments later, Chemah came out to the living room, once again prepared to address his children. Michelle was sitting on the couch with Tatsuya on her left and Héro on her right. Both children looked as if they could have been born to Michelle. They looked up at her with reverence and the love only a child can give unconditionally. Michelle looked like a queen holding court.

"A lady in the street and a freak in the bed" is what most men were looking for. Michelle surpassed that. She was his hope, his dream, and his salvation.

Chapter 24
The Gingerbread Man

Victor was out of breath as he reached the doors of Mount Sinai Hospital. He had reached the store thirty minutes ago after attending a full day of classes and received the news that his mother had been taken to the hospital at around eleven o'clock this morning. That was a full hour after he'd left the house and now here it was, five o'clock in the evening, and he was just finding out that his mother had been ill. Miss Dorothy, the lady who owned the beauty salon next door, had manned the counter for his mother after she had been found lying unconscious on the grocery store floor and the ambulance had taken her away. The beauty salon owner, who had known Victor since he was a little boy, had explained to him upon his arrival that she had not known where any of the keys were kept. Otherwise she would have closed the store up for the day. She had taken care of all their customers for the last six hours, and the receipts of the day and all the money she had taken were in the cash register.

Victor knew where his mother kept the keys. Now he was torn between leaving Miss Dorothy the keys and running out the door to find out what was going on at the hospital, or staying the extra five minutes to close the store properly. He decided quickly that his mother would have wanted him to close the store himself. He profusely thanked the woman who had been his mother's friend for years and set about closing the store.

Victor approached the information desk and asked which way it was to the emergency room. He was directed to follow the painted red footprints on the floor to his right and was told they would lead him directly to the emergency room. Victor ran down the hall, following the painted footprints as they made him change direction twenty yards down the corridor. Victor felt a stitch in his side, he had still not recuperated from the run he had made from the train station to the hospital. He had been running from a lot of things lately, ranging from the cops to his responsibilities to his family. Victor heard the old nursery rhyme in the back of his mind: *Run, run as fast as you can, you can't catch me, I'm the gingerbread man.* It was time to stop running, Victor thought. As he turned a corner and picked up speed, the anxiety to learn his mother's condition overwhelmed him.

Thirty seconds later Victor slammed through the emergency room door. Everyone in the waiting area looked up when they heard the door bang open. Most of the patients waiting looked beaten and forlorn. They looked at Victor expectantly, and when he did nothing more extraordinary than rush over to the triage nurse, everyone went back to their own business.

"How can I help you?" the nurse asked, without looking up from her paperwork.

"I'm looking for Ms. Reesey Brown. She was supposed to have been brought in a few hours ago," Victor said sounding unsure of the information he was providing.

The nurse was a short Filipina woman who appeared to have no patience for patients. She looked up momentarily and asked, "And you are…?"

"I'm her son, Victor Brown," he said, suddenly aware of his disheveled appearance as the nurse scrutinized him from behind her glasses. The nurse seemed to stare at him for a lifetime before taking a moment to look down at one of the ten clipboards on her desk.

"Excuse me one second," she said, getting up from behind her desk and disappearing behind the double doors through which incoming urgent cases were whisked.

Victor waited patiently for several minutes until the nurse came back. When she approached Victor, he knew she did not have good news.

"Your mother was taken to the psychiatric emergency room," she told

Victor bluntly. "Have a seat. The doctor will be out in a moment to talk to you about your mother."

Victor was stupefied to find out that his mother had been taken to the psychiatric emergency room. From the information Miss Dorothy had given him, he thought maybe his mother had had a coronary or stroke. She had, after all, been found unconscious in the store.

After a thirty-minute wait among the blind, crippled, and crazy who inhabited the emergency room, Victor heard his name whine through the tinny P.A. system. "Mr. Brown, please come to the nurses' station. Mr. Victor Brown, please come to the nurses' station."

Victor got up from his seat and went back to where the Filipina nurse was sitting. There waiting for him was a tall blond man who stood behind the nurse. Victor guessed that this was the doctor he had been waiting for.

"Mr. Brown?" the blond man asked, extending his hand over the counter for Victor to shake. "I'm Dr. Foqua."

Victor shook the man's hand and was instantly repulsed by how soft and sweaty it was. "How is my mother, doctor?" Victor said, getting right to the point.

"Why don't we step inside where we can talk in private," the doctor said, directing Victor to come around the counter and follow him through the double doors.

Once through the doors, the doctor led Victor past some of the emergency room patients who had been called while Victor had waited. They continued a short way down a corridor and toward a small door that read Psych ER. Victor followed him through that door, which opened into a room about a quarter of the size of the regular emergency room. Victor noticed that some of the seats had handcuffs attached to them and shuddered to think that someone might have handcuffed his mother to one of these chairs.

Victor continued to follow the doctor through a final door that had the name "Gerald Foqua, M.D." written on it. The room was small but comfortable. There were only two chairs in the room and they were both large and comfortable. The doctor sat down in the chair that was behind the desk and motioned for Victor to take the one in front of him.

The doctor reintroduced himself to Victor. "I'm Dr. Foqua, chief of Psychiatry here at Mount Sinai." Victor didn't respond to the doctor's claim to the title of chief of Psychiatry. He sat up straight, prepared to listen closely to anything the doctor had to say.

"Your mother was brought into the ER today because she was found unconscious in her place of business." Victor nodded, indicating that he was following him so far. "When she came to, your mother was asked very simple questions that she was unable to answer. A stroke-induced memory loss was instantly ruled out with a CT and an MRI." Dr. Foqua took a deep breath and crossed his legs before resuming his narrative. "As luck would have it, I was in the ER with a colleague when your mother was being referred to the psychiatric emergency room. Trying to avoid congestion in the area that I'm ultimately responsible for, I decided to interview your mother myself."

Victor was growing impatient and decided to interrupt the doctor. "Sir, where is my mother right now?"

"Your mother is a very sick woman, Mr. Brown. This afternoon I decided to admit her to the ward."

"You admitted my mother into a psych ward?" Victor raised his voice. "On the basis of what did you do that? She wasn't a danger to herself as far as I know, and she hasn't been a danger to anyone else, has she?" Victor asked.

"It isn't as simple as that, Mr. Brown," the doctor said patiently. "Your mother's CT scan showed some abnormalities, but was inconclusive. So I decided to check your mother's cerebrospinal fluid for evidence of abnormal neurotransmitter levels. Once again, it was a good thing that I was on hand during the process, because another doctor might have missed it. On a hunch I interviewed your mother further myself and when I got the results back from the CSF study, I was able to make a diagnosis. That's what took me so long before I saw you. I didn't want to make a premature diagnosis."

"So what is it that you believe she has, doctor?"

The doctor seemed to come to life with this question, as if he'd been waiting his whole life for a case such as this one. "It is my belief that your mother has a dissociative identity disorder." The doctor made the announcement as if

Victor should stand up and clap when he said it. Victor's look told the doctor that he didn't have a clue as to what he had said.

The doctor continued, "That in itself is a rare diagnosis. The thing that makes your mother's case even rarer is that I believe it was caused by a neuro-chemical reaction induced by alcohol consumption."

"I don't know anything about this dissociative whatever."

"Dissociative identity disorder," Dr. Foqua corrected him.

"Right, the identity disorder," Victor placated him. "Your theory doesn't really make sense because my mother is not a heavy drinker. As a matter of fact, she's a church-going woman and although she does have an occasional drink, most of the time the only alcohol that she consumes is the communion wine at the church."

With the last sentence that Victor uttered the doctor became excited again. "Then that's it, I was right. The only reason that your mother has lasted this long without a breakdown is because she has only been ingesting a thimbleful of alcohol at a time. Although a thimbleful of alcohol will adversely affect anyone with such a neurochemical sensitivity, it would not likely consume them all at once. Tell me, Mr. Brown, have you noticed that your mother acts strangely, possibly doing things that are out of character for her after she takes the communion at church?"

Victor thought for a moment, wanting to answer the question that might help his mother, but thought better of it. Now that he knew that his mother's behavior was caused by a mental illness, his guilt weighed even heavier on him. When Victor didn't answer, the doctor asked him a second question. "Did your mother recently ingest more than the normal quantity of alcohol that she is accustomed to having?" Again, Victor thought about the party a few nights ago and how his mother had drunk two glasses of wine before he had left for the party himself.

"That could explain the reason for the breakdown that she had today," Dr. Foqua surmised. "If she drank one or two glasses of wine a few days ago, her synapses may now be burned out and the neurotransmitters that cause the disorder in her were probably released in larger amounts than her brain could handle, similar to what happens when someone takes ecstasy. When you take ecstasy, you feel so great because you have an excessive release of serotonin and epinephrine and naturally occurring opioids, all neurochemicals that make you feel euphoric. In your mother's case, the amount of these neurotransmitters is probably even in excess of what someone experiences on ecstasy and they are reeking havoc on her personality, her behavior, and her perceptions of the world around her."

Victor was reeling. His brain was deciphering everything that the doctor was telling him and then adding it to the equation that was his life. "Doctor, can you tell me some of the symptoms of this disorder?"

The doctor looked like he was about to lose his composure, but remained a consummate professional. He reached across his desk and grabbed a thick book that was on top of a small pile of papers. The title of the book read *DSM IV: The Diagnostic and Statistical Manual of Mental Health.* The doctor leafed quickly through the book. He handed it over, holding it open the page he wanted Victor to see. "You seem like a smart enough young man, here, read this."

Victor grabbed the open book and read the passage that the doctor pointed to.

Dissociative identity disorder is characterized by the presence of two or more distinct identities or personality states that recurrently take control of the individual's behavior, accompanied by an inability to recall important personal information that is too extensive to be explained by ordinary forgetfulness. It is a disorder characterized by identity fragmentation rather than a proliferation of separate personalities. NOTE: Individuals may meet the criteria for mood, substance-related, sexual, eating, or sleeping disorders.

Victor read the passage twice to make sure that he understood everything. He read the note in the passage three times and grimaced as he read the words mood and sexual disorders. It was all becoming very clear to him now.

"Dr. Foqua, is it possible that I might have this same disorder?" Victor asked.

"Well, Mr. Brown, that was something I was hoping to ask you about. Sometimes these disorders are genetic and are passed along from one family member to the next, and can be exhibited through any of the numerous characteristics of the disorder. Now as far as I can tell from talking to you, you don't have any of the traits of dissociative identity disorder, but that doesn't mean you don't have a neurochemical reaction to alcohol. Why, you may have a different variation of this alcohol-induced disorder or you may not have it at all. The range of symptoms is wide and you could meet one of the criteria or you could meet them all. What I'm trying to say to you, son, is that you never know with these things."

The thought that he could be predisposed to this disease scared Victor, but right now he had to think of his mother. "Doctor, when do you think I can see her?"

"I'm afraid it's going to be a few days, Mr. Brown. We'd like to stabilize her first, before we allow her any visitors."

"I understand, doctor." Victor got up from his seat, glad that he would not be able to see his mother. He didn't know how he would face her now that he knew that his sins were more culpable than hers.

He'd pray on it tonight after he went out one final time. He thought that tomorrow he might even admit himself for tests to see if he was susceptible to what the doctor had presented to him. That would definitely have to be tomorrow. Right now, he couldn't help himself. He felt driven to go out one last time. His past was slowly catching up to him. He knew tonight the race would be won or lost. He was hearing the rhyme again as he passed through the hospital's electronic sliding doors: *Run, run as fast as you can, you can't catch me, I'm the gingerbread man.*

Chapter 25
STRUMMING MY FACE WITH HIS FINGER

Michelle left her room and took the two steps to reach the opposite wall from her doorway. From there she went right, feeling along the wall the next few steps until she got to Chemah's bedroom. She pushed the door open slowly, knowing that Chemah would awaken instantly with the sound that the door made. She knew he would have gathered his wits by the time she reached his bed. She had never been in his bedroom and didn't know the layout the way she now knew the rest of the house. As she entered the bedroom she listened keenly for the sound that Chemah's breath would make. That sound would guide her into his arms.

Chemah had been awake and reading with the light on, but Michelle would not have known that. Chemah watched her come carefully into the room and he silently put the book that he was reading onto the nightstand. Michelle had been asleep in the bed when he had returned from his day out with the children. It had only been ten o'clock at night and he was disappointed that she was not up waiting for them when they'd gotten home.

Now as she entered his room three hours later, he wondered if she had slept in order to be fresh for this hour.

Michelle was wearing a white negligee cut low at the bodice to show the sloping of her ample breasts. The negligee was long and flowing around the ankles. Chemah unwittingly held his breath after a gasp passed his lips. The sight of Michelle's body revealed through the negligee as she came closer to his nightlight was breathtaking.

Michelle stood at the side of Chemah's bed with her arms at her side allowing him to enjoy the sight of her. She could now feel the heat of his nightlight and knew he had a perfect view of her. She waited for some sign that he approved and received it as he finally allowed himself to breathe again after a sigh escaped his lips.

Michelle's face looked innocent and unsure in contrast to her body. She was not used to being soft and feminine for a man. She was used to taking and being taken. According to the philosophies she had expressed in the past, making love was for those who believed in a perfect union. Until recently she did not believe it could exist for her. She was still reluctant to believe it now, but the way she felt herself fitting into this family that had adopted her so easily gave her pause to give it a try.

Michelle felt her belly quiver as Chemah pulled the string at her waist that held her negligee together. She heard the bed creak, then felt his breath against her face as he stood in front of her. Her exposed nipples extended a full inch from her breasts, and Chemah leaned in just enough that his bare abdomen barely grazed them. They stung him with their heat, but he endured it without pressing himself farther into her, as his body yearned for him to do.

He was purposely torturing them both with his reluctance, wanting to be sure that she was in tune with what his mind and heart needed, before he committed his soul to her forever.

Chemah closed his eyes and allowed his hand to find a path from Michelle's waist up to her face. His hand burned with the need to stop and knead her flesh along the way, but he would not allow himself that pleasure until the time was right. Chemah used the back of his hand to caress Michelle's cheek and she could not stop herself from emitting a throaty, purring sound as she tilted her chin upward to expose more of herself to him.

Chemah couldn't wait anymore, but he had to hear the words before he went further.

"Do you love me?" he whispered into her ear.

Michelle felt the tears burn her cheeks at the shame of denying him this for so long.

She sniffed and sobbed into his hand, as her head nodded yes to his question.

"Tell me," he demanded of her, not allowing her body to speak her mind.

Michelle's body convulsed as she cried and sobbed into Chemah's hand. Her body was experiencing the catharsis of her long-held low self-esteem. In order for her to be with him, she had to find herself worthy. It had taken a long time for her to get there, but she had arrived.

"I—*sob*—love—*sob*—YOU!" Michelle said, each word punctuated by a guttural sound totally unfamiliar to her ears.

Chemah didn't wipe her tears away. Instead, he bent his head forward to touch her lips with his, so that she could taste the tears that fell from his eyes, as he tasted hers. It was a communion for the soul.

Minutes later, Michelle found herself crying again. This time she didn't know why she was crying. She had never had this experience before. Chemah had spread her legs with the weight of his body and had entered her gently, even though the hardness of his manhood told her that he wanted to be much more forceful. Her Venus had welcomed him by bathing him in preorgasmic moisture when their pubic bones touched. Chemah kissed her gently again and her whole body broke into a sweat. Venus was clasping and unclasping without Michelle's permission and then the tears came. Michelle's whole body convulsed repeatedly as Chemah spasmed inside of her time and again.

The whole episode was over in minutes, but years later the couple would remind each other how they had made love for hours on that fateful day.

As they fell asleep in each other's arms, the house creaked and settled around them. Chemah welcomed the sounds that told him he was home, but realized that he had never felt more at home than he did in Michelle's arms right now.

Chapter 26
WHOSE HOUSE?

It was nine o'clock on a Tuesday morning and already Michelle was up and working on new material. She had begged off walking the children to school with Ms. Richmond so that she could work on her craft. Ms. Richmond understood, and conveniently announced that she would be picking them up from school by herself because she wanted to take them with her to the library. She said she would have them back for dinner. Michelle thanked her, knowing that Ms. Richmond was only trying to keep them out of her hair for the afternoon. She had attempted to get some work done yesterday, but with the kids around it had not worked out.

She loved those kids, but if she were going to come up with a new routine, this afternoon would have to be all business.

The weekend gigs had gone so well that the producer of another show had approached Michelle afterward and offered her work at the club he was booking for.

Michelle knew that Chemah didn't like the fact that she was moving away from his scope of control very quickly, but when they spoke openly about it on the way home, he confided that the Street Sweeper had not struck again when they had deduced that he would. Chemah proposed to her that after this long period of time, he may have simply decided to stop the killing.

In truth, Chemah knew from experience that serial killers never "simply decide to stop killing." They could move on to better hunting grounds, they could get caught, or they could die, but they never just stopped. He knew that

Michelle would leave his protection soon enough and didn't want her to have any more anxiety than she had to before she made the decision.

Chemah had gone to work early this morning. His captain had called him directly and informed him of an anonymous tip. The informant had given an address in Queens where the Street Sweeper could be found. The captain sent a patrol car over to the address, with instructions to stop anybody that was leaving the home. If no one was seen leaving, they were to sit tight and wait for the two detectives to arrive. It was probably a crank call, but he had to check every lead that was introduced.

Chemah called Keith's cell and told him not to come directly to work this morning. He knew Keith lived in Queens and that was where the address that they had been tipped off to was located. Chemah thought he'd spare him the trip all the way into Manhattan and gave him the address and time where they should meet. It had been thirty minutes since Chemah kissed Michelle good-bye and left the house.

Michelle was getting comfortable on the couch when she was startled by the sound of a key jiggling in the door lock. She knew it couldn't be Chemah. He was already well on his way to work. The thought crossed her mind that Ms. Richmond might have decided to come over, but dismissed the thought, knowing that Ms. Richmond always knocked even before she used her key.

The serenity that she had found in the safe haven that Chemah's home provided was gone and her paranoia was back. *The killer has found me,* she thought, wishing she had waited a little longer before letting Base out in the backyard. Momentarily, she was frozen in place by her fear, but her survival instincts took over and she attempted to jump up from the couch, with the intention of barring the door with the weight of her body. Unfortunately, she jumped up too quickly and lost her bearing. Her first step sent her tumbling over the coffee table in front of her and before she could recover, whoever was using a key to enter the house was standing in the open doorway and letting in a steady stream of cold air.

Margarita had used her old set of keys to enter the house that she had bought and paid for, before she had ever met Chemah. She had worked alongside the contractors to renovate this home and would never think of it as anybody else's but her own. Chemah had won the house in the divorce settlement, but that was because she didn't fight for it. She'd wanted her daughter to have a good place to grow up and the only way that Chemah would agree to stay here with her daughter was if she relinquished all rights to it. At the time, she had almost lost all hope of ever being free again and decided to sign the house over to Chemah, against her lawyer's counsel.

When Margarita was released from jail, the house keys were in the property that was returned to her. She remembered that she still had them, when Chemah refused to talk to her and had denied her the right to visit her own daughter. She didn't care that it violated her parole, she had the right to see her own daughter. She had taken a chance that Chemah might have changed the locks, but why would he? As far as he knew, the only other set of keys besides his own would have been safe in a penitentiary property storage department.

Margarita's plan was to wait in the house for Chemah to come home with her daughter. She knew the type of man Chemah was and was sure that he would not make a scene in front of their daughter that might scar her for life. All she wanted to do was see her and visit for a while. It's a mother's right, she rationalized.

Margarita closed the door and was walking toward the woman that was scrambling on the floor in the living room.

Michelle heard the footsteps coming toward her and tried to get behind the couch as her hands simultaneously looked for something hard to defend herself with. She made it behind the couch, but found nothing with which to help her fight. She felt the presence of someone standing over her and was preparing to spring upward, with the intention of using her head as a battering ram, as her West Indian father had once taught her.

"Hello, excuse me, are you all right?" Michelle heard the voice of the person standing over her. *It's a female*, she thought, almost fainting with relief.

Michelle stood up straight, using the back of the couch as support. Taking a moment to fix her blouse, which she could tell by the feel of it was riding up her back, Michelle gently sniffed the air and smelled what she considered to be a very expensive perfume. It was Angel, two hundred dollars for less than three ounces and only one store in the world sold it, Saks Fifth Avenue. This was no street hood come to rob the house.

"Who are you?" Michelle asked.

"I might ask the same of you," Margarita countered.

"You might not ask me who I am, when you're standing in my house," Michelle said, raising her voice for emphasis.

Margarita cocked her head curiously to the side, realizing for the first time that the woman in front of her was blind. "*Your* house, huh?" she said, half-amused by Michelle's response. She circled around to the front of the couch, and Michelle followed the sound of her stiletto heels on the hardwood floor. Michelle held her position behind the couch, not wanting to take another misstep and appear even more vulnerable than she had appeared earlier, cringing on the floor.

"That's funny, I didn't know Chemah had remarried," Margarita said dryly.

Michelle heard a confidence in this woman's voice that she didn't like. She heard the cushions adjust, and knew that the woman had sat down on the couch. Michelle still didn't move from what she considered a vantage point. At least now there was something between her and this intruder. She knew that if she followed the back of the couch straight to the end, and continued to run straight another five yards afterward, that she would reach the front door. She knew the woman had heels on, that might give her a chance to get to the door first.

"Miss, I don't know who you are, but if you don't leave here right now, I'm going to call the police," Michelle threatened.

"Well, if you really are the owner of this house and you and Chemah are married now, then he must have spoken to you about me at some time. My name is Margarita Smith Rivers. I thought about getting rid of the 'Rivers' part after the divorce, but I've invested so much into it that, like this house, I find it hard to give up."

Michelle had had to catch herself. She had almost put her open hand to her mouth in shock when the female intruder had revealed her name. It would have been a sure giveaway as to how scared she actually was. If the intruder was not lying and she actually was who she purported to be, then Michelle really was in a room by herself with a killer. Ms. Richmond had told Michelle the story of how Margarita had killed Tatsuya's mother and then tried to kill Chemah when he found out her secret and attempted to arrest her.

"That's impossible, Margarita Smith is still in prison," Michelle said, feeling so nervous now that she felt her stomach start to bubble so that it made a loud whirring sound. Michelle felt like she had to pass gas, but sucked in her stomach and clenched her butt cheeks to stop herself.

"I guess Chemah forgot to tell you that I recently got out of prison and I've come back to be with my family. You obviously aren't part of his inner circle, poor dear, otherwise you would have known."

Michelle's discomfort was obvious to Margarita and although she didn't find it especially funny, she forced herself to giggle, letting Michelle know that she knew she was the cause of her gas attack.

"Maybe you should go use the bathroom, little girl," Margarita taunted her. "I'll wait here by myself until Chemah comes back." Margarita's taunt incensed Michelle. She was not used to being talked to in this manner.

"I don't care who you are," Michelle said, reaching into her back pocket. She had forgotten that she had put her cellphone there earlier, after telling Rhonda to phone her directly next time she wanted to talk business, instead of using Chemah as an intermediary. Margarita sat up straight when Michelle flipped the phone open. It would not do to have the police come in here and drag her out for violating her parole.

"You have five seconds to get the fuck out of here or I will make sure that if you are Margarita you don't see your daughter for—hmm, let's see—I'd say another five years."

Margarita knew that Michelle was not bluffing. She had already dialed two numbers and Margarita guessed that they were nine and one. Michelle held the phone in front of her with a finger over the final one and started to count. "One, two…"

Margarita's voice and the sound of the couch adjusting stopped Michelle's count. "No need to act childish, child. I'm leaving." Michelle followed the sound of Margarita's heels as they moved toward the door. "Tell Chemah that I stopped by and that he should be expecting a call from my lawyer."

Margarita turned the doorknob and opened the door wide. If not for the fact that her reflexes were still sharp from protecting herself and the others under her care in the prison system, she might have lost all her teeth. Instead, she was able to turn her head just in time for the fist that came at her head with a killing force to glance her jaw. The jolt of the punch was enough to rock her brain against her skull. A bright light went off in Margarita's head and she fell backward, smashing into the couch.

Michelle heard Margarita's stumbling footsteps and then felt her crash against the couch. She assumed that Margarita was trying to rush her. Her finger was still hovering over the last digit to be dialed for her 911 call and she pressed it.

Chapter 27
THE LOST SOULS

Keith Medlin had quickly subdued and handcuffed Michelle to a bed upstairs. Something had told him to bring two rolls of tape with him today, and he was glad that he did. Keith hadn't intended to help two souls be released into heaven in one day, but he was doing God's work and even if he had to work with them all day, he knew he could get them to pray with him to release their souls.

He had rushed back downstairs to Margarita, who he thought might wake up before he got a chance to tape her up. He had carried her downstairs carefully, not wanting her to wake up to any more pain than she had to before it was her time.

Keith had been at Chemah's front door, about to stick the key into the lock that he had made from Chemah's house keys, when Margarita opened the door for him. If he had known it was going to be this easy, he would have never taken the trouble to rush to the locksmith to have a key made the day that Chemah had left him in the car outside of his children's school. It had only taken ten minutes, but he didn't know if it would have been worth it if Chemah had come out and found that he had driven his car.

Keith had recognized Margarita immediately. When he was at the detectives' training program reading through all of Chemah's old cases, he had read the file that described how Margarita had slept with a police captain while married to Chemah in order to deceive them both.

Even then, he had fantasized how he would have made her repent for the sins that she committed. For a while, it had bothered him that she was living it up in jail, without having God to answer to, but he tried not to let it bother him, knowing that God works in mysterious ways. Now here she was delivered to him, as if in answer to a prayer. It reassured him that he was doing God's work.

Even as he finished taping Margarita's legs, he realized that in his haste and happiness in dealing with Margarita he'd made a careless mistake. He could hear Michelle upstairs kicking the headboard, trying to escape. He wasn't afraid that she would get away. He knew that her attempts would be futile. It was the damn handcuffs that he had used for the sake of speed. If she kept it up they would leave marks that would easily be identified as handcuff marks. Although anybody could buy a pair of handcuffs, he knew that there were certain elements that would be traceable. He knew that Chemah would leave no stone unturned to find him, once he performed his duty to God.

Keith left Margarita half-taped, lying on the basement floor, and started bounding up the stairs. He took the steps two at a time, but was not even winded when he reached the second landing. Keith rushed toward the open door of the room where he'd left Michelle, but stopped abruptly at the doorway when he saw the figure of another man kicking the bedpost, trying in vain to break the well-made structure

"Victor?"

Victor turned around when he heard his brother whisper his name. "Keith!"

"Victor, what are you doing here?" Keith asked.

"I'm here to help you," Victor responded.

Keith smiled proudly at his little brother and took the three quick steps to stand directly in front of him. Keith wrapped his arms around his brother before Victor could get his arms up to defend himself. He had him in a bear-like grip and had picked him up off the ground as easily as you would a child. "I knew you would want to be a part of this, little brother, I just knew it. God has a purpose for both of us," Keith said gleefully, gently putting Victor down. "How did you know how to find me?" Keith asked, as if they were standing in the middle of a picnic.

"I saw the pictures of the victims in the newspaper, Keith, they were taped up the way we used to play in the alley behind the store. I remembered the day you caught little Rhaheem stealing from the store. How you dragged him to the back when Momma wasn't around. I helped you tape him up, remember? You made me take my turn beating him. You said God doesn't like thieves and that we were helping God. It only occurred to me yesterday for the first time that we did that right after coming from church."

Keith smiled fondly at his little brother. "Yeah, we were doing God's work, even back then." Keith's mind was sick, but it wasn't addled; he came right back to the subject at hand. "But how did you find me here?" Keith used his forefinger to stab down at the floor. He was starting to look at his younger brother suspiciously.

"I know where you live," Victor said matter-of-factly. "After you left Momma's house five years ago, I tracked you down through the Internet. It wasn't that hard. I always wanted to know that you were all right. Momma would have wanted to know that you were okay. Every now and then I would stand in front of your building, hiding behind cars to watch you come out. Momma forbade me to ever talk to you again, but that didn't mean I couldn't come see you.

"After your third victim was found, I tried to follow you so that I could prove to myself that it wasn't you who was doing the killing. I kept losing you, but I always had an idea of where you would end up. You used up all our old stomping grounds and hideouts. The police and I would always arrive there at around the same time. They thought it was me doing the killing."

"Yeah, we've been watching you for a while now," Keith confessed.

"You knew I was a suspect?" Victor asked.

"Of course I knew, I'm the number two detective on the case. But they could never have pinned it on you, could they, because you were never guilty. Of course I was the only one that ever knew that."

"It was only bad luck that I always figured out the places you were taking your victims too late to stop you."

"To stop me? I thought you said you were here to help me," Keith said slowly, backing away from his brother.

"I am here to help you," Victor said pleadingly. "Momma got sick yesterday. She collapsed and they say she has a mental illness caused by a neurochemical imbalance induced by alcohol consumption. I think that's what you're suffering from, too."

Keith's eyes were bright with madness and he laughed. "You're the one that's crazy, little bruh. I don't even drink."

"That's why it all makes sense," Victor tried to explain. "I know you still go to church every Sunday. It's the communion wine that's causing the imbalance. If you were drinking any more than that, the neurochemical imbalance would have taken you out long ago. It's the small amounts that are making you crazy."

The smile went out of Keith's face. "Crazy? You think it's crazy to help God rid this world of these sick, disease-infested bitches? The kind of whores that took our father away from Momma. You weren't the one that Daddy used to take with him, telling Momma he was going to take me to the park. I was the one who would sit waiting and watching television in some whore's parlor, listening to the rutting noises in the next room, until Daddy was finished doing his 'good deed,' as he'd call it. For 'the women who simply can't help themselves.'"

"It's only that type of women that I help cleanse the world of, Vic. It's what God wants me to do."

"And what about this one, Keith, what about the one downstairs?" Victor asked.

"These two are especially evil," Keith said with conviction. "This one," he said, pointing to Michelle's still-struggling form on the bed, "could identify who I am. I wasn't going to do anything to her. I merely watched her, to make sure she wasn't telling the police anything more than they already knew. But as I watched her I realized that it was God's hand that brought me to her. She fornicated with four different men in a week while I was keeping an eye on her. You see, she hasn't realized that God was sending her a message by taking her sight away, telling her to change her ways before it was too late. But while I watched, I realized God was telling me it was already too late for her and it was my job to bring her to Him.

"The one downstairs, I just figured out myself. She fornicated outside of her marriage and killed a good woman. Killed a woman that was taking care of her child without a man by her side, like Momma did with us. I asked God for her when this all started and He's delivered her to me, as His faithful servant."

Victor listened to his brother and knew there was no way he would be able to talk him down from his euphoric hysteria. It was exactly as the doctor had described last night.

Instead he reached into his back pocket for the gun that his mother had always kept behind the counter in the store. Keith saw his brother reach and went for his back pocket at the same time. One shot rang out from Victor's gun, hitting Keith in the shoulder before Keith was able to bring the full force of his hammer down squarely between his brother's eyes, killing Victor instantly. Keith winced from the pain in his shoulder as he leaned over his brother's dead body and spoke to him for the last time.

"You were misled, brother, you were misled."

Chapter 28
911

Chemah was more than halfway to his destination in Queens when he got the phone call from the precinct. It was the sergeant of the day, Paul Jordan, he and Chemah had come on the job together.

"Hey, Chemah, I thought I should call you to give you a heads-up because the boss informed us this morning that you were following up a lead on the Street Sweeper case. The switchboard got a nine-one-one call about thirty minutes ago from a cellphone. The caller hung up the phone before we could answer it, but when we checked the number it turned out that it was the same woman that you had interviewed a month ago on the Street Sweeper case. I sent a car over to her apartment right away, but I got a call back from the patrol car and they said that no one was home. I even had them break in the door in case someone had her hostage inside, you know. Fortunately, there was nothing going on, no sign of a struggle, nothing."

Chemah thanked the sergeant for the information and got off at the next exit.

Before getting back on the Grand Central Parkway to go back toward Manhattan, he took a moment to put the siren and lights on in his car. He dialed the number to his home phone, but it did as he had expected, it only rang. He turned the car around and went as fast as he could. He was shaken. He didn't know Michelle's cellphone number. And why would she need her cell if she hadn't left the house? "Shit!" he said out loud. She had promised him that she wouldn't leave the house alone anymore. Either he or Ms. Richmond was to be with her at all times outside of the home.

"Promises were meant to be broken," he could hear her saying to him later. Right now he had to make sure she was all right. Keith would have to handle the Street Sweeper tip without him. He'd call him as soon as he got back to the house.

Chapter 29
DON'T CALL IT A COMEBACK

Keith was bent over Michelle, unlocking the handcuffs. He was trying to formulate a believable explanation in his mind as to how he had gotten to Chemah's house too late to save Michelle and Margarita. He hated to desecrate his brother's body anymore than he had to, but he would have to shoot him in the head again to make the story believable. If he had any luck at all they wouldn't do an autopsy to find out how he had actually died.

The pain in his shoulder and his concentration on securing Michelle with only one of his arms working was going to be his undoing. He had taken too much time with Victor and Michelle and had forgotten about Margarita.

Earlier Michelle had wondered what had happened to Margarita. Now she smelled the Angel perfume again and heard the stealthy footsteps that Keith could not and thought it conceivable that she might still be rescued. Michelle continued to struggle against Keith, hoping that she could distract him enough to keep him from hearing Margarita as she could. Michelle knew that Margarita was almost right behind him and wondered what she was waiting for.

Margarita had regained consciousness three minutes ago when she'd heard the gun go off. She had come to full alertness almost instantly and ripped off the tape around her legs without much problem. Her first instinct was to run out of the house quickly and get some help. But she remembered the blind girl in the house and fought bitterly with herself about leaving another woman helpless to fend for herself against the jackals of society that preyed on the weak. She hadn't done it in prison and she wouldn't do it here.

Margarita tiptoed up the basement stairs and stopped at the kitchen to get a knife. She went up the stairs quickly and silently, letting the noise coming from upstairs be the beacon that brought her to the party.

Margarita was standing behind Keith, surprised that she had gotten this close to him without him hearing her. She saw the hammer that he had dropped on the floor and gingerly picked it up, feeling comfortable with the weight of it in her hands. Now she had two weapons. A hammer in her left hand and a butcher knife in her right. Margarita waited another moment for Keith to extract one of Michelle's hands from the handcuffs before she cleared her throat: "Hhrrmmff, eshcuse me, I think you dropped shomethin'," she said, talking through the side of her mouth. It was only through trying to talk that she realized that her jaw was broken. The realization that she was looking at the man who had done it set her eyes ablaze.

Keith saw the look in her eyes and the weapons in her hands. "Fuck," he said, turning to swing at her wildly with his only good hand. Michelle stepped back to avoid the back hand and it gave Keith the opportunity to get to his feet. Margarita stood her ground, refusing to back up again. She held the two weapons high in each hand and waited for Keith to take another step. Instead of stepping, Keith attempted to head fake her, hoping that she would step to the right and away from the doorway. Then he could run back down to his work bag where he had left his firearm.

Keith's fake backfired. It caused Margarita's fight-or-flight response into action and now she was in fight mode. She didn't use any special technique, but the one she had used the few times she had fought in her neighborhood. Everybody who couldn't fight always did the Windmill. Margarita closed her eyes and started swinging wildly with both arms. She felt two punches land, one over her eye and another crushing her nose, but she kept swinging through the attack. Margarita felt the hammer landing and the knife rendering flesh time and again, but didn't open her eyes or stop swinging her arms until only the air contested the arcing of her weapons. When she opened her eyes again, the man who had attacked her lay broken and mangled on the floor, a bloody mess. His face, which she was sure had been handsome before, was no longer recognizable. Only one hand was still attached to his body. That was probably the hand he had not been able to lift against her.

Margarita looked over to Michelle, who was sitting up in the bed, appearing to be listening for something. "Ish ovah," Margarita said, unsuccessfully trying to sound like a heroine through her broken mouth.

Margarita turned and stumbled out of the room. She had to get downstairs and to a phone to call the police.

Before Margarita reached the bottom of the stairs that led to the living room, the front door flew open and Chemah sprang into the room, looking around wildly.

Margarita took the final two steps that took her into the living room and broke into the biggest grin that her broken jaw would allow her. She was so happy to see him that she almost wept.

To Chemah, Margarita appeared to be a crazed, blood-soaked killer, still carrying her instruments of revenge. The fact that she had killed the first woman that he had ever loved quickly became an issue.

"Noooooo, what have you done?" Chemah screamed at Margarita.

It was then that Margarita realized that she had not dropped the hammer and knife. She looked at her fist closed around the weapons and her blood ran cold. Margarita no longer had the ability to talk. Her jaw was almost hanging from her face now. As Chemah came rushing toward her, Margarita's one good eye went wide with fear. Her hands finally released the two weapons she was holding and she took no notice that they hit her feet. The hammer had probably injured her big toe, but she could not move.

When Chemah reached her, both his hands went immediately around her throat. He intended to choke the life out of her. Margarita was making a gurgling sound, as the ability to stand left her. It didn't seem to bother Chemah that he had to hold up all of her weight with just the strength in his arms. He kept her face level with his, determined to see the life in her eyes go out. It would be hard to do with the tears that stung his cheeks, filling his eyes over and over again, but he'd make the adjustment, so he'd have a fond memory of this moment.

"Chemah, is that you? Thank God you're here."

Chemah looked up toward the stairs at the sound of Michelle's voice and thought he was looking at an apparition. He could see her feeling her way down the stairs. Ghosts didn't do that, he thought. He allowed Margarita to fall to his feet with a loud thud.

Margarita grasped her throat and gasped for air. That was enough indication to Chemah that she would be all right.

Chemah grabbed Michelle before she put her foot on the last step and smashed her against his chest. He kept squeezing her and squeezing her until she finally had to taken another breath. "Chemah, Chemah, I'm all right, I'm all right."

Chemah pushed her away from his chest and looked at her from head to toe to make sure that she was telling the truth. When he was satisfied that she was fine, he started to breathe normally again.

"Where's Margarita, Chemah? She saved my life."

"Saved your life from what?" Chemah asked, startled.

"The Street Sweeper. He's upstairs."

Chemah's eyes went to the staircase, but before he could move, Michelle answered his question. "He's dead. Margarita killed him. And there's another man, too. I don't know who he was, but he tried to save me. They were talking like they were brothers."

Chemah let go of Michelle and went back to Margarita, who was very still. He felt for her carotid artery. She still had a pulse, but she was unconscious.

Chemah pulled out his cellphone and called for an ambulance. He waited with Margarita until the ambulance came, in case he had to give her mouth-to-mouth resuscitation. When the EMTs came and took over, they assured him that all her vital signs were stable and that she would be okay. Michelle had argued with him, but he made her go to the hospital, too, to make sure she was all right.

Chemah finally went upstairs and was shocked to see his partner lying on the floor, ripped to shreds. He called his captain and explained what he guessed had transpired. Fifteen minutes later the captain was on the scene and they pieced the story together. Chemah would have to explain to the Internal Affairs Division what he was doing with a witness in his house. They would also want to know how his partner had managed to do these killings right under his nose. He could only explain half of it, the rest of it he'd make up as he went along.

Chemah finally went upstairs and saw the two bodies that Michelle had described. One of the bodies was lying face down and the other was staring straight up at the ceiling with the one eye that was still left in his head.

It took Chemah a moment, but he was startled when he realized that the person lying in front of him was his partner. Chemah fell to one knee immediately and searched for a pulse on Keith's neck. When he found none, he opened his phone to dial 911 again, but thought better of it.

The captain would be here soon and if he called in an officer down or in need of assistance it would only alert the media to the crime at his home that much sooner.

Chemah stood up and walked over to the body that was face down. He gently pulled the body toward him and was surprised to see Victor's face. Chemah would have sworn on a stack of Bibles that this young man was not the killer and yet here he was lying dead in his home, next to his dead partner.

The immediate evidence indicated that Keith had somehow stopped Victor from killing Michelle and then was attacked by Margarita. Chemah remembered the gruesome tools that Margarita had in her hands when he had accosted her earlier. It was for sure that she was the one who had killed Keith, but why?

Victor's only visible wound was a cracked skull. Chemah looked around for any weapon or object that could have caused such a wound, but there wasn't one in clear sight. It was possible that Margarita had somehow killed them both, but no. Michelle said that Margarita had saved her from the killer. It was possible that Michelle was wrong. After all she couldn't see and she might have gotten confused.

Fifteen minutes later when the Captain arrived, Chemah was finishing his preservation of the crime scene. He had posted officers at the front door and had given instructions that no one but the captain and the medical examiner be allowed to enter the area.

Chemah showed the captain upstairs to where the bodies still lay and they went over the evidence together. They knew there were missing pieces, but the only reasonable answer they could come up with without those answers, was that Margarita had killed an officer of the law while he was in the act of apprehending a known killer.

The captain concurred with Chemah when Chemah admitted to prematurely letting Margarita go to the hospital without first placing her under arrest.

While Chemah worked with the Medical Examiner to ensure the crime scene was preserved and the two bodies could be pronounced dead with a probable cause, the captain radioed the dispatcher. He had two officers take Margarita into custody when she arrived at the hospital.

"Let's go," the captain said to Chemah.

"To the hospital?

"Where else? You think I'm going to let you go to the hospital alone to arrest your ex-wife for the murder of your partner?"

"I don't see why not." Chemah shrugged and walked out toward the captain's car.

"Yeah, you wouldn't." The captain followed him toward the car. "Why not your car?"

"I've got a good parking spot and you have to come back here anyway."

The captain tossed Chemah the car keys. Chemah was surprised, but he caught them.

"Yeast infection again?"

The captain nodded.

‡‡‡

Columbia Presbyterian Hospital started as a small facility in a primarily

Jewish community known as Washington Heights in upper Manhattan. It was now one of the foremost primary care and research facilities in the country as well as a major medical school. It was hard not to get lost in a place this immense. But Chemah and the captain had been there so frequently that they made their way through the hospital and to the emergency room without ever showing their credentials.

When they reached the emergency room they were informed by the triage staff, who knew them both well, that Margarita was taken upstairs to the OR after being seen by the chief of plastic surgery. Apparently, he was an old friend of Margarita's and she asked for him to be paged as soon as she was brought into the emergency room.

Chemah asked for Michelle and was informed that she was escorted to the OR waiting room by the two police officers who showed up to take Margarita into custody.

Michelle was sitting in the waiting room between the two officers when Chemah and the captain entered. The two officers stood simultaneously and Michelle looked toward the doorway where they stood. The captain gave the officers a nod and they both left the room quietly to wait right outside the door.

"Chemah?"

Chemah came immediately to Michelle's side and kissed her softly on the cheek. The captain made a grunting noise. And Chemah didn't know if it was the yeast infection or the sight of him kissing their main witness that bothered him.

"Chemah, the officers told me that they were given orders to arrest Margarita. Is that true?"

"Yes, it's true; she killed a New York City Police detective. She has to be arrested."

"But, she saved my life, Chemah, how can that be?"

"You must have gotten confused in all of the commotion, Michelle. Margarita killed the man that was in the room trying to rescue you"

"No, you have it wrong. The man that was trying to rescue me was the brother of the Street Sweeper. They talked a long time before the Street Sweeper killed him. It was his younger brother by the story they passed between themselves. One brother stayed home with mom, the other was on his own for a long time without the family."

Chemah and the captain looked at each other and finally shared a shocked look of understanding.

"There was gunfire and a sound of metal hitting bone. It was the Street Sweeper that was left standing," she continued.

Chemah pointed to his shoulder, unnecessarily indicating to the captain the one place they had found where Keith was shot. The captain nodded his head and ran his fingers through his hair nervously.

"Afterward he was talking to himself about how his brother had not understood. He mentioned you, Chemah, like he was helping you. You were his hero."

Chemah listened to the rest of the story; he and the Captain sharing glances that confirmed they were drawing the same conclusions.

Chemah was going to have to explain to the internal affairs division what he was doing with a witness in his house. Chemah knew the captain would not leave his ass hanging in the wind on that issue. What would be really hard to explain was how his partner had done these heinous killings right under his nose without him having a clue. He could only explain half of it, the rest of it he'd make up as he went along.

Epilogue

The newspapers had a field day with the whole story. Margarita was a hero to the whole city. The mayor gave her a citation as the Citizen of the Year, while she was still healing in her hospital bed a month after the whole ordeal was over. Margarita had refused to take any pictures until her face had totally healed from the plastic surgery she had undergone the day after her harrowing ordeal. The plastic surgery she needed on her face was taken care of by many philanthropic battered women's organizations. She received a reward for information leading to the capture of the Street Sweeper and decided to use it on a down payment for her choice of cars, the Jaguar XJ6. When she went down to the dealer they gave her the car for free, as a promotional gimmick, as long as she did a photo op in front of their store. She did the photo op and drove her new car straight to Chemah's home to pick up her daughter.

Tatsuya stood still as a statue, holding Michelle's hand in a viselike grip, as he watched his father hand his baby sister over to the woman who had killed his mother. Chemah had to explain to him numerous times over the past few days why Margarita was entitled to visitation rights. Tatsuya couldn't or wouldn't understand why.

Once Chemah adjusted the child protection car seat in Margarita's Jag, he put Héro in it gently and kissed her good-bye. Chemah gave Margarita twenty different instructions on what Héro liked and disliked and Margarita had enough sense to act as if she were actually listening.

Héro had no qualms about leaving. She was quite happy to see the lady that always treated her nice when they visited at the other place. Chemah had unnecessarily assured her that she would be back at the end of the day. Héro laughed and waved to him as Margarita sped away.

Chemah walked back to the house where Michelle and Tatsuya waited at the door. Chemah kissed Michelle tenderly on the lips and she kissed him back just as gently. They had found peace with each other this past month. They were supposed to spend the day moving the rest of her things to the house, but now he thought maybe they'd just take Tatsuya out somewhere. He knew Tatsuya was upset and he wanted to do everything he could to make him feel better.

"Anybody for ice cream?" Chemah suggested to the two as he ushered them into the house.

Michelle gave a shiver of disgust. "Is that your answer to everything?"

"It's too cold, Dad," Tatsuya piped in.

Chemah shrugged his shoulders and smiled. He knew he had done all he could.

ABOUT THE AUTHOR

David Rivera, Jr. has been writing short stories for many years and has been inspired by the writings of the contemporary black male writers who have emerged during the past few years. His first book, *Harlem's Dragon*, has been received with great enthusiasm by other writers as well as literary critics. David lives in Harlem, U.S.A. with his family and aspires to reignite the literary flame that Harlem had been renowned for with his novels *Harlem's Dragon* and *The Street Sweeper*. He received a bachelor's degree in sociology and a master's degree in public administration. David Rivera, Jr. can be contacted at setodavid@aol.com. Visit his web site at www.davidriverajr.com.

Printed in the United States
By Bookmasters